"Carole!" Stevie cried. "I've got to talk to you!"

Carole grinned at her irrepressible friend. "This is Stevie Lake," she told Lisa. "And Stevie, meet Lisa Atwood, who's joining our class."

"Oh, right, the new girl," Stevie said.

"What's so exciting?" Carole asked Stevie. Stevie jumped right into a long explanation about her parents and her grades at school. Lisa realized that she knew the Lakes. They lived in her neighborhood—at the nicest end of it. Lisa thought Stevie was funny and seemed like a lot of fun.

"I think I'll *die* if I can't go on the trip!" Stevie exclaimed. "I mean, I've already chosen the jeans I'm taking and I've been having dreams about campfires and mountain trails for months! Right? You have, too." Carole nodded. "So, anyway, I've got this scheme—I know, I *always* have a scheme, right? But this one'll work. It'll make me a fortune. I'll never have to do another math project again as long as I *live*!" Then, without taking a breath, Stevie switched gears. "Welcome to Pine Hollow, Lisa. You're going to love it. This place is just full of traditions." And before Lisa could ask her what she meant, Stevie disappeared into one of the stalls.

If you love ponies, you'll love . . .

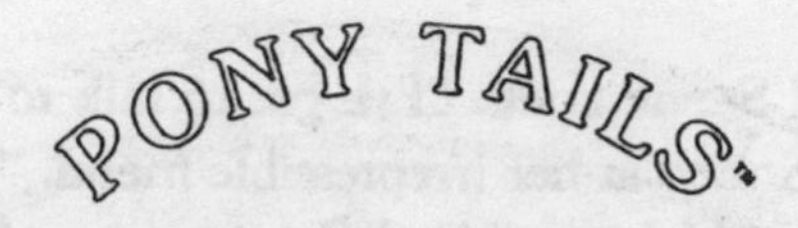

Saddle up for fun and adventure with three pony-crazy kids in this terrific new series from Bonnie Bryant, author of the successful *The Saddle Club* series.

Join May, Jasmine and Corey, three girls with a passion for ponies, as they form their own club called the Pony Tails.

Don't miss the first titles, coming from May 1996.

1. PONY CRAZY
2. MAY'S RIDING LESSON

COMING SOON:

3. COREY'S PONY IS MISSING
4. JASMINE'S CHRISTMAS RIDE

HORSE CRAZY

BONNIE BRYANT

A BANTAM BOOK®
TORONTO • NEW YORK • LONDON • SYDNEY • AUCKLAND

THE SADDLE CLUB: HORSE CRAZY
A BANTAM BOOK : 0 553 17650 1

I would like to express my special thanks to Michelle Deudne, Carol Kiger and Mary Swearingen.
B.B.H.

First publication in Great Britain

PRINTING HISTORY
Bantam edition published 1989
Reprinted 1989, 1990 (three times), 1991, 1992, 1993, 1994 (twice)
Reissued 1996

Bantam Books are published by Transworld Publishers Ltd,
61–63 Uxbridge Road, Ealing, London W5 5SA,
in Australia by Transworld Publishers (Australia) Pty Ltd,
15–25 Helles Avenue, Moorebank, NSW 2170,
and in New Zealand by Transworld Publishers (NZ) Ltd,
3 William Pickering Drive, Albany, Auckland.

Printed and bound in Great Britain by
Cox & Wyman Ltd, Reading, Berkshire

For Marilyn E. Marlow

". . . AND THAT'S *FINAL,* Stephanie!" The words echoed in Stevie Lake's ear long after her mother had closed her bedroom door. She knew her mother meant what she had said. When Mrs. Lake's mind was made up, she was every bit as stubborn as her daughter.

Stevie flopped onto her bed. "I hate it when she calls me Stephanie," she grumbled. Her cat, Madonna, settled down at the foot of the bed. Absentmindedly, Stevie stroked the cat. She had some serious thinking to do.

Her parents had told her in no uncertain terms that if she didn't improve her grades, she wasn't going on the horseback riding camp-out next month. Unless Stevie proved she was a responsible student, her parents certainly weren't going to pay for this treat.

"Treat" was an understatement, Stevie thought. The Mountain Trail Overnight was the grand finale of the year. She'd been talking about it for months with her friends at the Pine Hollow Stables, especially her best friend, Carole Hanson. They'd even already decided what to pack! There was no way she was going to miss that camp-out. She just *had* to go.

Stevie sighed. She knew she could do well in school when she put her mind to it. She wasn't dumb, she was just more interested in having fun than doing schoolwork. Math did give her a bit of a problem, though. It was Stevie's bad luck that she had a math project on decimals and percentages due in three weeks for the quarter term grades—right before the overnight trip. There was no way she could do a math project good enough to improve her grade.

Possibilities raced through her mind. She considered basing her project on her younger brother Michael's guppies. She could count how many more appeared in the tank each day. Too boring, she decided.

She could do some work for her dad's business that had to do with decimals and percentages. But then, Stevie considered the consequences if she made a mistake for her father. So, that was out, along with the guppies.

It seemed hopeless. Suddenly Stevie realized that her mother hadn't said she couldn't go on the overnight trip if her grades didn't improve. She had just said that Stevie's parents woudn't *pay* for it.

If her parents wouldn't pay for it, Stevie could pay for it herself! Stevie had a few dollars in her frequently raided piggy bank, but definitely not nearly enough to pay for the overnight trip. Her allowance was usually gone a few days after she got it. Her twin brother, Alex, said the problem was that there were too many days in a week for Stevie's allowance. Stevie knew she couldn't do anything about that, so that meant saving up for the trip was out.

But she could *earn* money for the trip, Stevie thought excitedly. There must be a zillion things people needed to have done that they'd pay her to do. She'd never tried to earn money before, but lots of other kids did it, so it couldn't be too difficult.

Stevie's active imagination began working. She could see herself helping people carry groceries from the store. She could walk dogs. She could baby-sit. She could help her friends with household chores they didn't want to do. She could water plants for people on vacation. The possibilities seemed endless.

She was roused from her thoughts by Madonna's insistent meows at the bedroom door. Stevie hopped off the bed and opened the door for Madonna. The cat zipped out of Stevie's room and set off down the hall, swishing her tail disdainfully. Stevie, suddenly cheerful now that she had a plan, went down to the kitchen to help her mother with lunch. For as soon as lunch was over, it would be time to get ready for her riding class. And that was definitely something to be happy about. Besides, Carole would be sure to have more ideas for money-making schemes.

Things were definitely looking up.

CAROLE HANSON WAS already at Pine Hollow Stables. Her father, a Marine Corps colonel stationed at Quantico, near Washington, D.C., had afternoon duty that day. He could only bring Carole to Pine Hollow in the morning. He had apologized for dropping her off at her riding class two hours early, but Carole assured him that she didn't mind at all. She loved every minute she spent there. It was just about perfect.

Carole loved the stable area where Pine Hollow's twenty-five horses lived. The stable area was U-shaped, with the horses' stalls in double rows on the long sides of the U. The short side of the U housed saddles and bridles in the tack room, equipment such as grooming aids and pitchforks in the equipment room, and grain and a few bales of hay in the feed room. Carole could spend hours going from stall to stall, patting the horses, chatting with them. She could, that is, except for one thing: Max Regnery.

Max owned the stable, which had been passed down from his grandfather to his father, and then to him. On the surface, Max seemed sort of relaxed and laid-back, but it was well-known among the riders that idleness bothered Max. Carole was welcome to hang around the stable—as long as she was doing something useful.

Today, she was cleaning tack. She had a saddle on the stand in front of her and she applied the saddle soap with a damp sponge and rubbed it gently in circles. She admired the shine the soap brought out in the worn leather.

Like Stevie, Carole Hanson was twelve years old. She was a slender girl, with an intense look in her dark brown eyes. Her wavy black hair usually fell loosely to her shoulders, but when she rode in a horse show, she made a single braid in the back and pinned it up. Carole was totally committed to horses and planned to own her own stable when she grew up.

Even though her friend Stevie hadn't gotten to the stable yet, she wasn't alone. While Carole worked, she chatted with Max's mother, affectionately known as Mrs. Reg.

"Dad just kept apologizing to me today about having to bring me here so early. These days he's always telling me he's sorry about something. . . ."

"Well, perhaps he is, Carole," Mrs. Reg said gently.

Carole thought about that for a minute. It was true that her father had been sorry, and really sad, ever since her mother had died six months earlier from cancer. So had she. They both missed her very much.

"But it's more than sad, Mrs. Reg," Carole said.

"I know that. I think your father does, too. But I think what he's sorry about is that he can't be both a mother and a father to you."

"But that's silly," Carole protested. "I don't expect him to be."

"Try telling that to him," Mrs. Reg said.

Carole buffed the saddle for a few minutes, considering how she might assure her father that he wasn't letting her down.

"Mrs. Reg," she said finally. The kind woman looked over at her. "Have you ever heard the expression, 'Tell it to the Marines'?" Carole asked wryly.

Mrs. Reg laughed and nodded. "Okay, then, you'll just have to wait. He'll learn, Carole, he'll learn."

Carole picked up the clean saddle and carried it over to its rack. Then she reached for the bridle, which hung on the bracket above the saddle rack.

"When you finish that bridle, I need you in the ring," Max called brusquely as he strutted past the tack-room door. He was leading Patch, a black-and-white pinto, toward the indoor ring. Carole paused to watch. Max and the horse were followed by a girl who looked familiar to Carole, and a woman who appeared to be the girl's mother. The girl was slight, with wavy brown hair and a little ski-jump nose, which was sprinkled with freckles. She had a look most people would call cute, but her eyes seemed to see beyond the surface. One glance and Carole could tell she was smart.

Carole suddenly remembered the girl's name. It was Lisa Atwood. She went to the same school Carole attended, Willow Creek Junior High School, but she was a grade ahead of Carole. Carole had barely recognized her, though. At school, Lisa had the confident look of a straight-A student—which she was. Honors Day at the junior high was really more like Lisa Atwood Day. But here, at the stable, Lisa looked decidedly uncomfortable. Carole decided to finish soaping the bridle quickly so she could see what was up.

LISA RELUCTANTLY FOLLOWED her mother into the riding ring. She felt like a fifth wheel. Mrs. Atwood was having a lively conversation with Mr. Regnery about horsemanship. She was telling him about this wonderful rider who had so much natural talent, but just a bit of schooling, who wanted to be his student. She told him about the rider's devotion to the sport and the hours spent reading about equitation.

"In fact," Mrs. Atwood said, "just the last time she rode in a show, she got a blue ribbon."

With a start, Lisa realized her mother was talking about her. *She* was supposed to be this naturally skilled, intensely interested rider. The show her mother was talking about had been a pony ride at the zoo when she was four years old. *All* the kids who didn't cry had gotten blue ribbons!

Lisa sighed. The thing that Lisa was the best at was school. But it seemed that her mother wanted her to be the best at absolutely everything else. Lisa took ballet class on Mondays, painting on Wednesdays, tennis on Fridays, and now seemed to be fated to go riding on Saturdays and Tuesdays. She didn't really *mind* this frenzy of activity, but it seemed a little ridiculous to her.

And sometimes, like now, she felt a little embarrassed. She and her mother had spent hours last weekend at the riding store, purchasing the outfit she now wore. Lisa was in riding breeches, with shiny black leather boots up to her knees. She had on a white cotton shirt and a necktie. (Mrs. Atwood had insisted on buying a tie with horses on it. She wouldn't even let Lisa borrow a striped one from her brother.) Lisa was also wearing a black jacket, slightly flared at the hips. On her head, she had a black velvet-covered hard hat. To complete the outfit, Lisa carried a pair of brown leather riding gloves. She may have looked ready to enter the ring at New York's famous Madison Square Garden, but she felt like an imposter, dressed for Halloween.

Max Regnery waited quietly while Mrs. Atwood continued her one-sided discussion about Lisa. He held Patch's reins with his right hand. Lisa stood to his left. While Mrs. Atwood chatted, Max turned toward Lisa.

Lisa was sure he thought she was weird. She felt her face reddening. And then, while Max was nodding sagely at Mrs. Atwood, he winked at Lisa.

He knew! He knew her mother was stretching the truth. And that was all right with him. When Mrs. Atwood finally stopped talking, Max turned to Lisa.

"Have you done much riding, Lisa?" he asked.

"Just ponies at the zoo, and once at day camp. I mean, I know how to walk and how to stop the horse," she said, ignoring her mother's glare.

"Okay, then, we'll see what you learned at the zoo," he said. Then he showed her how to mount Patch and, within seconds, she was on the horse.

"Good," Max said approvingly. She felt wonderful. Being in the saddle was okay, but what was wonderful was that this man didn't take her mother's silliness seriously, and he didn't mind that she really didn't know much about horses. Lisa felt more relaxed than she had since they'd arrived. Maybe riding wouldn't be so bad, after all.

Just then, a girl entered the ring. She was wearing riding breeches and high boots like Lisa's, but they had long ago lost the sheen of newness. Somehow, this tall slender girl looked comfortable in her riding clothes—not costumed, the way Lisa felt.

"Lisa," Max said, "I'd like to introduce you to Carole Hanson." He pointed to the girl. "Once our young riders are past the introductory level, they're grouped more by age than skill. You'll be in Carole's class so I thought you should meet now."

"We already know each other, Max," Carole said. "We go to the same school."

Lisa looked at her in surprise, then recognized the seventh-grader. At school, Carole always seemed to be disorganized, papers flying around, pencils trailing from her book bag. But here at the stable, Carole seemed completely at ease and full of confidence. Lisa found her very likable—the kind of girl she'd like to have for a friend. Maybe horseback riding would be fun after all. Somehow, Carole's confidence was contagious and Lisa caught it.

"Okay, now, show us your stuff," Max said. "Begin with a walk."

Lisa took the single reins in her hands and nudged Patch with her heels. The horse began walking. It was a slow, rambling pace, comfortable and natural. After she'd circled the ring three times, Max asked her to trot. She didn't know how to make a horse trot, but it seemed that Patch understood the word, for he immediately began a bouncy trot. Almost instinctively, Lisa began rising and sitting with the horse's pace, more to get away from the bouncing saddle than anything.

"Good, good," Max said. "Now walk again." The horse slowed to a walk. It didn't seem particularly extraordinary to Lisa, but she could see that her mother was beaming with pride.

Just at that moment, another girl came through the door from the outside into the indoor ring, letting the door slam loudly behind her.

Patch, like all horses, had a long memory for things that spooked him. Fireworks spooked Patch, and even though he couldn't see any flash of light, a sudden loud noise was just as bad. At the instant the door slammed, Patch took off with Lisa aboard.

First, Patch bucked. Lisa grabbed the front of the saddle with her right hand and held on for dear life. At least when Patch started galloping, she had a good grip. At first, Lisa was afraid she would fall off, and then, she began hoping she would. Patch tore around the ring so fast, Lisa could barely tell where she was. Walls, doors, people, all merged into a blur. There seemed to be no way to control the horse.

She heard Max calling to her, telling her to relax—or was he saying it to Patch? It didn't matter. Neither of them was relaxed. Patch kept circling the ring and Lisa kept holding on. And the pounding of the horse's hooves continued in a very fast-one-two-three beat. It was like a waltz at top speed.

Lisa could waltz. She'd taken ballroom dancing for three years. She began to sway with the horse, shifting her weight in the saddle with the rocking of the pace.

Now; instead of feeling like a helpless sack of flour, she was riding! She was in control. Lisa let go of the saddle and put gentle pressure on the reins. Instantly, Patch responded, slowing his pace. Apparently, he was no longer spooked and was ready to behave. He switched to a trot. She pulled the reins again, and the trot changed to a walk. Lisa brought him over to where her mother and Max stood with Carole. Her mother was white-faced. Carole's look was one of frank admiration. Whoever it was who had slammed the door was nowhere in sight.

Max reached up to help Lisa dismount from Patch. "That must have been some zoo!" Max said.

MAX DISMISSED THE girls, asking Carole to show Lisa around. Lisa followed her and Patch back to the stall area while Max and Mrs. Atwood talked before the class.

The Class. It would be Lisa's first class and she wasn't sure she liked the idea of it. She was still feeling a strange mixture of fear and pride from her ride on Patch.

"What made him go crazy like that?" Lisa asked.

Carole glanced around uneasily and then shrugged. "Most horses *do* have things that frighten them, which you try to avoid. Some don't like dogs. Some jump when they see something waving. Patch doesn't like loud noises. See, when something scares a horse, he remembers it for a long time—especially if it happened when he was young. They may learn in the meantime that the thing *isn't* dangerous, but they still never forget that fear from long ago."

Although it was odd, it made some sense. After all, even though Lisa was confident that she'd handled Patch well when he'd run away with her, she knew it would take her a long time to forget how scared she'd been. Perhaps she had something in common with these big animals after all. But if everybody knew Patch was afraid of loud noises, why would someone have slammed the door and caused her such trouble? Lisa was too shy to ask and Carole didn't offer an explanation.

While they walked Patch to his stall, Lisa looked around her. There were stalls on either side of the long skylit passageway. Each stall had a window on the outside with a door-gate three-quarters high—just high enough for the horses to look over. The horses watched Lisa and Carole passing them with Patch.

"Horses are curious animals. They like to be able to see what's going on," Carole said. "That's why stalls always have windows and doors the horses can see over."

Carole slid open the door to Patch's stall and led him in. She handed Lisa the reins to hold while she loosened the girth on the saddle. Lisa looked in Patch's eyes, expecting to see some resentment. There was none. The horse's dark eyes seemed almost sleepy and certainly contented. Lisa patted Patch's soft nose tentatively.

"You'll be riding him in class," Carole explained.

"It's easier to leave the tack on him, and he doesn't mind, as long as he can get some water." Carole checked to be sure there was fresh water. She slipped a halter over his bridle and snapped ties on either side of the halter so he couldn't roll in his stall and tangle his tack. Then she patted Patch on the neck and the two girls left the stall, sliding the door closed and locking it behind them. Lisa noticed that the stall had a standard sliding latch as well as a key chain-type clip.

"Is that really necessary?" Lisa asked.

"Just watch," Carole said. As if on cue, Patch stuck his head out over the top of his door and began nuzzling the sliding latch. Within seconds, the horse had grasped the bolt and was working at it. "Horses are natural door openers. Never give one a chance—he'll take it, and you'll be in big trouble. Okay, next stop is the tack room."

Just then, a nearby stall door slid closed and was latched. Carole tried to lead Lisa past the girl who had emerged from the stall, but the girl's look was commanding.

"Lisa Atwood, this is Veronica diAngelo," Carole said, introducing her to the pretty girl with smooth black hair. "She's the—"

Veronica interrupted Carole. "So *you're* the new student!" she said.

It surprised Lisa that anybody knew she was there. She didn't know what to say to Veronica, so she just stood there awkwardly while Veronica's eyes took her in. It took only a few seconds. Lisa felt as if she were being analyzed by some twenty-third-century ultra-beam. When Veronica's smile warmed from automatic to sincere, Lisa knew she'd passed. She didn't know why.

"How's Cobalt?" Carole asked, gesturing toward the horse behind Veronica. Lisa turned to look. Even with her untrained eye, she knew this regal-looking horse was special. His shiny coat was coal-black. His bright eyes sparkled and his head nodded invitingly. Carole walked over and rubbed his forehead affectionately.

"He's fine, as you can see," Veronica said off-handedly. "Would you like to exercise him tomorrow?" Carole nodded eagerly. "Good. Then let's talk after class to make arrangements." There was something almost threatening in Veronica's voice, Lisa thought, but she couldn't imagine why that would be. Carole seemed so nice. Veronica turned to Lisa. "I'll see you in class," Veronica said, and walked off.

The girls continued along the hallway toward the tack room. As they progressed, they met some of the other students, but it all happened so fast, Lisa couldn't remember any of their names until Stevie Lake came running up to them.

"Carole!" she cried. "I've got to talk to you!"

Carole grinned at her irrepressible friend. "This is

Stevie Lake," she told Lisa. "And Stevie, meet Lisa Atwood, who's joining our class."

"Oh, right, the new girl," Stevie said. Lisa wondered how she had known. Could she have been the one—

"What's so exciting?" Carole asked Stevie, interrupting Lisa's thoughts. Stevie jumped right into a long explanation about her parents and her grades at school. Lisa realized that she knew the Lakes. They lived in her neighborhood—at the nicest end of it. They had a big house on the corner with a pool in the back yard.

She'd seen Stevie around, but she'd never met her. Stevie went to a private girls' school in the neighboring town. Because Lisa knew their house, and knew that Stevie went to the exclusive school, she knew the Lakes were fairly wealthy, but she never could have guessed it by looking at Stevie. Stevie was wearing an old, worn pair of jeans and some cowboy boots that looked as if they'd seen better days—*lots* of them. Stevie caught her eye. Embarrassed, Lisa looked away. She realized she'd been looking at Stevie almost the same way Veronica had looked at her. She didn't want to be rude to Stevie. In fact, Lisa thought Stevie was funny and seemed like a lot of fun.

"I think I'll *die* if I can't go on the trip!" Stevie exclaimed. "I mean, I've already chosen the jeans I'm taking and I've been having dreams about campfires and mountain trails for months! Right? You have, too." Carole nodded. "So, anyway, I've got this scheme—I know, I *always* have a scheme, right? But this one'll work. It'll make me a fortune. I'll never have to do another math project as long as I *live*!" Then, without taking a breath, Stevie switched gears. "Look, I'll tell you all about everything later," Stevie went on. "I've got to groom Comanche before class. Welcome to Pine Hollow, Lisa. You're going to love it. This place is just full of traditions." And before Lisa could ask her what she meant, Stevie disappeared into one of the stalls. Lisa laughed to herself. She'd like to be Stevie's friend, but if it meant following crazy conversations like that, it could be exhausting!

"Is she always like that?" Lisa asked.

"Always," Carole assured her, smiling broadly.

But somebody like Stevie could be the kind of person who would slam a door when Patch was in the ring. What kind of friend was *that*?

"Coming?" Carole asked Lisa. "Tack room's this way." Obediently, Lisa followed her to the end of the corridor.

The first thing Lisa noticed in the tack room was that it appeared to be very disorganized. Endless tangles of leather straps hung on the wall, and saddles seemed to be everywhere. The second thing she noticed was the smell. The rich, pungent leather smell mingled with the earthy smell of the horses themselves. She brea deeply.

"It's great, isn't it?" Carole asked her.

Lisa nodded, smiling. "But how do you know what tack to take for each horse?" she asked.

"Oh, it's all completely organized," Carole assured her. "You just have to get used to the system. Also, in here are hard hats for riders who don't have their own like you do." Carole pointed to a large wall where about forty black velvet-covered hard hats of all different sizes hung on nails. Lisa stared at the wall for a second. Carole did a double take.

The hats weren't just hanging on the wall. They were, in fact, carefully arranged so that they spelled "MTO!" Carole burst out laughing.

"What's that?" Lisa asked.

"That's Stevie," Carole said as if it were an answer to the question. "What I mean is that Stevie did it. She's always doing fun things like that. She thinks that the hat wall is a sort of message board, too. Anyway, MTO stands for Mountain Trail Overnight, which is an overnight horseback trip next month. You'll hear more about it soon. Stevie's excited about it already. Actually, so am I."

Lisa wondered if she'd be able to go on such a trip. Would she want to? Would her mother *let* her go? It seemed odd to Lisa to realize that only a half an hour ago, she was dreading climbing on a horse, and now, after one hair-raising ride, she was already thinking about an overnight trail ride. But she didn't have much of a chance to think about it anymore. Carole was all business on her tour of the tack room.

Carole showed Lisa the tack she had soaped earlier, which they would now put on Delilah, the horse Carole would ride in class.

"Delilah—that's a funny name." Lisa laughed.

"Wait'll you see her," Carole said, leading her back out to the row of stalls. This hall was on the other leg of the U from where Patch was stalled. Delilah, it turned out, was a luscious creamy palomino with a long silvery mane. Her name really fit her. She *looked* like a flirt. But she didn't act like one. She was clearly a high-strung creature and nervous around strangers. It didn't seem to bother Carole, though. She patiently went about her business.

In the next fifteen minutes, Carole showed Lisa how to put a bridle and a saddle on a horse. It seemed impossibly complicated to Lisa.

"I'm never going to remember the difference between the crownpiece and the headband—to say nothing of the cheek strap and the throatlatch!" she groaned.

"Oh, sure you are," Carole consoled her. "See, you already know their names. That's half the battle. Besides, the horses are pretty used to this process so they don't make a fuss. As long as you need help, one of us will give it to you. Then, when you don't need help anymore, you'll be able to give it to another new student."

"Oh, I don't know about that."

"It's one of the traditions around here, Lisa," Carole told her patiently. "We all help out. We help the stable and we help each other. It's a good way to learn. And, it helps keep the costs down."

"Oh, it's not that I *wouldn't* help another girl," Lisa said quickly. "It's just that I don't know if I'll ever be able to live up to that tradition!"

That was the second time Lisa had heard the word tradition. She had the feeling she would hear it often at Pine Hollow. But she did wonder how far one had to go to help other riders. Lisa was almost certain Carole knew who had slammed the door and frightened Patch. Why was she being so closemouthed about it? Who was *she* helping?

"You almost done in there?" Stevie Lake asked, peering into Delilah's stall, interrupting Lisa's thoughts.

"Almost," Carole said. "But do me a favor, huh? Can you get Patch ready for class and bring him to the mounting area for Lisa?"

"Sure," Stevie said agreeably.

Stevie left and Carole showed Lisa how to tighten the horse's girth—the "belt" that held the saddle in place. Delilah didn't like it at all. First, she'd take in a big breath so that when she let it out, the saddle was too loose. Then, she'd step away from Carole or bob her big head up and down. She even got Lisa cornered in her stall. Lisa was frightened, but Carole took it all in stride. As many times as Delilah tried to cause trouble, Carole spoke sharply to her and proceeded to tighten the girth. After six tries, the job was done.

It reminded Lisa of what it was like to look after her little cousins, ages two and four. She didn't much like doing that.

Finally, Carole led Delilah and Lisa to the mounting block in the outdoor ring. Patch was fastened to the fence, waiting for Lisa. She eyed him uneasily, but he seemed unconcerned. Lisa decided she should be, too—until she realized that she and Carole were practically the last ones ready for class. Max was across the ring, helping one student tighten the girth on her horse. Everybody else was looking at them. Lisa really didn't want everybody to watch her get back on the horse, but there was no way around it. She looked to Carole for instruction.

"Okay, here's what you do," Carole said. "First, see that horseshoe nailed on the wall?" Lisa saw it and nodded. "Well, that's one of our traditions here. It's the good-luck horseshoe. You have to touch it with your right hand before you mount your horse. Nobody has ever been badly hurt at Pine Hollow and the tradition is that it's because of the good-luck horseshoe." With that, Carole brushed the worn horseshoe with her right hand. Then, smoothly, she swept onto Delilah.

It was such a simple motion, done so gracefully, Lisa thought. She could do it, too. Mimicking Carole's gesture, she touched the horseshoe. Then, she held the reins in her left hand and prepared to mount, uncomfortably aware of the eyes that stared at her.

Something was wrong. She raised her left leg to where the stirrup ought to have been and tried to lift herself up, but it didn't work. Because there wasn't any stirrup there. Nothing to step on, nothing to hold her foot. She tried jumping up, but the horse was too high. She tried pulling herself up by the saddle, but that didn't work either because she couldn't get a good grip. She stared helplessly at the impossible task, tears welling in her eyes.

That was when she heard the first spurt of laughter. Through the blurry tears of frustration, she looked at the girls in the class around her. Each seemed to be smirking, some giggling, and one, openly laughing. Lisa's eyes met Stevie's. Stevie tried to control her laughter to meet Lisa's stare with mock seriousness. But her mirth bubbled over and she tried to smother her giggles by putting her hand over her mouth.

Lisa was beginning to get the feeling that there were some traditions at Pine Hollow that she wasn't going to like at all.

"NOW, LISA," MAX called firmly from the center of the ring, "I want you to sit more forward in the saddle. Tighten up on your reins. Don't *lean* forward. Relax your calf muscles. Heels down!"

Lisa tried, but following five directions at once wasn't easy.

"Shoulders back! And don't point your toes out. But relax those muscles!"

Make that eight directions at once. Lisa sighed. Things seemed to have gone from bad to worse ever since Carole had helped her replace her stirrups and she'd mounted Patch. She'd never make it as a rider and she didn't think she'd want to. In fact, she'd never wanted to. It was her mother who wanted her to ride.

Lisa decided that her mother could take the lessons from then on.

At last, Max focused his attention on someone else. Lisa could relax now that she was out of the spotlight. She looked around at the six other riders in the ring. Besides Carole and Veronica, there were Polly Giacomin, Betsy Cavanaugh, Meg Durham, and, of course, Stevie Lake.

Lisa could still feel the pain of Stevie's laughter after she'd intentionally left the stirrups off Patch. Lisa thought the kind of girl who would play such a mean trick on her was also the kind of girl who would slam a door when Patch was in the ring. After all, Carole and Stevie were good friends, so that explained why Carole wouldn't tell Lisa that Stevie had caused Patch to run wild. Lisa promised herself that she'd get even with Stevie. She had no idea how, or when, but she knew the time would come, and she'd be ready when it did.

"Okay, now, pair up!" Max called to all the riders. That meant that they were to begin riding two by two.

"Isn't this just the *most* fun?" Betsy asked Lisa as she brought her horse next to Lisa and Patch. "I love horses!" Lisa really couldn't think of an answer so she stared straight ahead.

"Good, Lisa. Much better," Max said. She liked the compliment, but Lisa had no more idea of what she was doing right than of what she'd been doing wrong.

* * *

USUALLY, STEVIE HATED it when Max had the class walk and then trot two by two. It meant the end of the class was near and she'd have to stop riding soon. But today, she didn't care so much because her mind was filled with plans. Before class, she'd talked to one of her neighbors about earning money and she had her first assignment: pool cleaning.

Also, she had to tell Carole about her plan. Carole could be flighty about some things, but when it came to horseback riding, she was all business. Earning money for horseback riding was part of that business. Stevie was counting on her help.

At Max's instruction, the horses began trotting. Class was almost over. All that was left was the soda whip—another of Pine Hollow's traditions. On the last trip around the ring, each rider grabbed a riding whip from a bucket. The rider who got the whip with the bottle cap attached to it was in charge of getting sodas for the rest of the class and her partner was in charge of putting her horse away.

"Hey, it's my turn for the soda whip!" Stevie called out as she grabbed at one of the whips in the bucket. No luck. It was just a whip. "Oh, drat!" Stevie said. The other girls in the class laughed.

"How come you want it today?" Carole asked her.

"I've got a job to do—remember I told you about how I've got to earn money?"

Carole nodded her head, but Stevie thought she looked doubtful. Stevie would show her that she could stick with *this* project!

In the end, it turned out that Lisa got the soda whip. Disappointed, Stevie dismounted and led Comanche back to his stall while Carole explained to Lisa what she'd have to do.

Lisa groaned inwardly, but she wasn't going to let Carole—or anybody else—think she was a bad sport. She readily relinquished Patch to Betsy and headed for the tack room, where there was a small locker area and the refrigerator.

Lisa was alone. All the other riders were with their horses. Mothers, fathers, and sitters waited in the office, which was in a separate building on the stable grounds. Suddenly, much sooner than she had expected, Lisa had her chance to get even with Stevie.

Usually, Lisa could shrug off something like this afternoon's incidents and maybe even laugh a little bit, too. But this time she just couldn't. She remembered vividly her terror as Patch tore around the ring. She could still hear Stevie's laughter and see the smirks from the other riders when Stevie had left off her stirrups. She could still feel the embarrassment.

There, on the floor, was a pair of sneakers belonging to Stevie Lake. Her initials were written all over them and there was nobody else in the class whose initials were S.L. So, before Lisa opened the refrigerator to get seven sodas, she took a minute—just a minute—to tie knots in Stevie's shoelaces.

When Lisa was younger, she'd been in the scouts—one activity which she had loved—and she'd learned every kind of knot there was. She did them all in Stevie's laces. Of course, Stevie would know who had done it. Lisa was the only one with the opportunity. But that didn't matter, because Stevie would also know she deserved it. A practical joker had to be prepared for retaliation.

Quickly, Lisa did her work, rendering Stevie's shoelaces useless for hours, unless she'd been a scout, too. As soon as she was done, Lisa grabbed seven sodas from the well-stocked refrigerator and delivered them to the riders who were untacking the horses. She was far away from the tack room when she heard Stevie's first yelp.

CAROLE WAS CLOSEST to the tack room when Stevie began screaming. She ran to find out what had happened. She found her friend standing in her socks with a pair of sneakers in her hand. The laces of the sneakers were all tied in an incredible set of knots, impossible to untie—and making it impossible even to separate the sneakers from each other.

"I don't believe this! And when I'm in such a hurry!" she wailed when she saw Carole. "Look at this mess! I can't go anywhere! And I can't wear my boots when I'm doing my job!"

Carole was used to Stevie's mood swings. She could be all sunshine one instant and thunderclouds the next. But the thunderclouds usually disappeared as quickly as they came. This time, they didn't. Stevie had told Carole about the job she was going to do. Carole had rarely seen her so eager to work. And now, at the very least, she was going to be late. This thundercloud wasn't going to disappear quickly.

Stevie went on howling about the knots. Within a few seconds, all of the riders were in the tack room, watching Stevie's temper display. Carole glanced at the girls. Most looked embarrassed at Stevie's outburst. A few looked sympathetic. Veronica stood by one door, masking a smile. Carole would have expected that.

Then Lisa appeared at the door. One look at her face and Carole knew she'd done it. Stevie, glaring at the onlookers, spotted Lisa at the same time. Her face had "guilty" written all over it.

Carole knew that Stevie could dish it out, but she didn't like to take it. It wouldn't occur to Stevie that Lisa hadn't liked the stirrup trick any more than Stevie was enjoying the shoelace trick. All Stevie would think of was that she had something important to do and she was going to be late because of this dumb joke. She began yelling at Lisa.

Lisa would have been perfectly happy to disappear into the ground. She hated being yelled at—almost as much as she'd hated being made a fool of without her stirrups. If she could have taken back the knotted laces, she would have—*if* Stevie also could have taken back the slammed door and the stirrup trick. While Stevie ranted, Lisa stood still. Then, when Stevie turned her attention to unknotting, Lisa turned on her heel and walked to the office, where her mother was waiting to drive her home.

Lisa slumped in the far corner of the front seat of the car. "I'm not going back there again, Mom. I don't want to learn to ride. I don't want to see those girls ever again. I don't want to ride another horse. I don't want to tighten saddle girths, slip bits into mouths, relax my calf muscles, look straight ahead, heels down, toes pointed in, shoulders back, forward in the saddle. Ever."

"Oh, darling, isn't it exciting?" Mrs. Atwood asked, almost breathlessly. "Max is such a dear and the horses are so nice. I'm just certain you'll be a wonderful rider, Lisa. Your father and I will be so proud of you. And, imagine—Veronica diAngelo is in your riding class. You will be her friend, won't you, dear?"

Had her mother heard her? Lisa wondered. Or, had she once again only spoken her doubts and her unhappiness to herself?

"You're so *quiet*, Lisa," her mother said, answering

that question for Lisa. "You *did* have a good time, didn't you, honey?"

Lisa knew that once again, she would just do what her parents wanted her to do. Once again, she'd be their good little girl, no matter what *she* wanted to do. Besides, her mother had made an interesting point. Veronica diAngelo *did* seem to want to be her friend. So, perhaps she could be Veronica's friend and ignore Carole and Stevie altogether.

For a moment, Lisa forgot about Carole and Stevie and thought about her gentle horse, Patch. All during class, Patch had been very sweet-natured, as if he understood her ignorance. In spite of herself, she had to admit that being on a horse was nice. It made her feel tall and powerful. And, much as she disliked Max telling her eight things to do at once, she'd loved it when he'd complimented her.

All right, she sighed to herself. She'd go again on Tuesday to the next class—and then she'd see. . . .

"CAROLE, CAN I borrow money for a phone call?" Stevie asked, hopping over to Carole on her one sneakered foot. She held the other sneaker, still hopelessly knotted, in her left hand.

"Sure," Carole said, reaching into her pocket for change. "What's up?"

"Well, I'm going to be late for my job. I'm supposed to vacuum the O'Mearas' pool. I thought I'd ask my brother Chad to do it for me. They've got a daughter I think Chad has a crush on. He'll like that. Then, I can go over to the shopping center and put a notice on that bulletin board. Good idea?"

"Sure," Carole said, though it seemed to her that Stevie would make more money by *doing* a job than by advertising for one. "Then I'll walk over there with you. I can get the bus from there."

"Great," Stevie said. "We can hang out for a while."

"Well, okay, but how's that going to earn you any money?" Carole teased. Stevie just shrugged.

After Stevie made her phone call and finished unknotting her lace, the girls walked the half-mile to Willow Creek's modest shopping center. Willow Creek was a small town about a half-hour drive from Washington, where most of the people, Stevie's parents included, worked. Since they were so close to the big city, they didn't have much of a shopping center. It had a variety store, a supermarket, two pharmacies, a jewelry store, an electronics store, a sporting goods store, a Tastee Delight ice cream parlor (TD's, as it was called by the junior high school kids who hung out there), and three shoe stores. It wasn't exactly a major shopping mall, but it was within walking distance of the stable *and* Stevie's house. Carole and Stevie had both spent a lot of time hanging out there after riding classes, especially since Carole's bus stopped there.

"I can't believe what that new girl, Lisa, did to me," Stevie said as they walked together to the shopping center.

"And what about what you did to her?" Carole asked.

"What I did to *her* was funny," Stevie said defensively.

"Funny to you, maybe, but not to her."

"Well, maybe, but playing a joke on a new kid is sort of a Pine Hollow tradition—"

"One I think we could do without," Carole interrupted. "Besides, didn't you hear what happened to her when Max was testing her?"

"No, what? Did she get some dirt on that fashion-model outfit she was wearing?"

"No, but she could have—or worse. She was on Patch and somebody slammed the door and—"

Stevie knew what happened when a door was slammed near Patch. "Oh, no! Patch took off? Who would do such a stupid thing? Did she fall hard?" Stevie asked.

"No. It was amazing. She stayed on!"

"No wonder Max let her into our class," Stevie said. For a moment she felt badly about her stirrup joke—until she remembered how angry she'd been about her shoelaces. And then they got to the shopping center and everything else was forgotten. Carole trailed Stevie into the supermarket and waited while she filled out a card for the bulletin board announcing she would do "odd jobs." She posted it with a pushpin. "Now, let's go to TD's," she said.

"First I want to stop at Sights 'n' Sounds. I think it'll be fun if I can get Dad a golden oldies tape—you know, stuff from the sixties when he and Mom were dating. I was teasing him about that stuff the other day. It turns out when he was in high school, he really wanted to be a rock star. He sang for me. I think it's a good thing he went into the Marine Corps instead!"

Giggling, the girls went into the electronics store together. Carole took a long time choosing a tape, trying to find one with the songs her father had been singing. While she riffled through the tapes, Stevie hung out near the counter, reading promotional material on televisions and stereos. Then she found a contest she could enter. First prize was a trip for two to Hawaii. She thought that would be fun. She was quickly lost in a dreamy image of herself riding bareback along the beaches of Hawaii at sunset, a handsome boy on the horse next to her. She wore exotic flowers in her hair. By the time she'd filled out the contest blank, she had put an imaginary lei around her neck and she could practically smell the sweet tropical blossoms.

"I'll take this one, please," Carole said, handing a cassette to the check-out woman. It brought Stevie right back to Willow Creek. A little disappointed to find herself so far from her tropical paradise, she shoved the contest entry slip into the cardboard box by the cash register and then waited by the door for Carole. A chocolate-dipped ice-cream cone would taste good—since she couldn't go to the luau she'd just daydreamed about.

* * *

CAROLE TOOK THE tape and stuffed her change into her pocket, following Stevie to TD's. Stevie paid for her cone and headed toward the outside tables behind the shop. Carole had to wait for her sundae and then dropped most of her change on the ground. Then she nearly dropped her ice cream while she picked up her money.

Stevie reappeared at the front of the shop in time to help Carole collect all her belongings.

"Sometimes I don't know how you make it through a day without me," Stevie teased.

"I wonder the same thing myself," Carole said, laughing at her own disorganization. "And I'll never make it through the MTO without you, so you'd better tell me more about this new business venture of yours."

As if on cue, Stevie was off and running—way off, as far as Carole could tell. Stevie was a great friend and all that, but her attention span was notably short. Carole didn't see how in the world Stevie could focus on earning money long enough to make the fifty dollars she'd need for this trip—particularly if she expected to do pool cleaning and garden work like hedge clipping! Stevie didn't know the first thing about hard work.

"Stevie!" Carole said when she'd finished. "Are you for real?"

"Sure am," Stevie said positively. "This is a new me, Carole."

"I don't want a new you. I liked the old one just fine. But wouldn't it be easier if you just got the old you to do a math project?"

"You know what kind of grade you get for counting guppies?" Stevie challenged. Carole had no idea what she was talking about. She stared blankly at Stevie. "C. That's what you get for guppies. And a C won't do me any good. I need at least a B-plus, preferably an A. So that's why I'm earning money."

"But what if you don't make enough to go on the MTO?" Carole asked. "You'd miss three wonderful days and nights of riding on a gorgeous mountain trail. We've been planning them for—"

"You don't think I can do it, do you?" Stevie was genuinely hurt.

"Well, it's not that," Carole protested. "It's just that . . ." Carole didn't know what to say. She didn't really believe Stevie could make fifty dollars cleaning pools and clipping hedges in three weeks. And, if she spent all of her time *trying* to earn the fifty dollars, she'd never have time to do a math project; and if she didn't do a math project *and* didn't make fifty dollars, she definitely wouldn't go on the trip.

Carole and Stevie had been talking about that weekend trip for months. It was the most important event of the year. It was what riding was *really* about. They had practically had their clothes packed for weeks! Now it seemed that their plans were falling apart and there was absolutely nothing Carole could do about it.

Carole took a bite of her sundae, but its gooey sweetness didn't make her feel any better. Stevie didn't seem to notice anything was wrong. She just began listing all the wonderful things she could do for people—for money.

". . . walk dogs, water plants, deliver newspapers, put up wallpaper, paint . . ."

Paint and wallpaper? Carole thought to herself. At this rate, Stevie would never make it to the MTO!

LISA STARED UNCOMFORTABLY at Pepper, the horse she was to ride in class that day, her second riding lesson. She held his bridle in her right hand, but she really had no idea how to put it on him, and while she looked at it and tried to figure out how it went, she only seemed to manage to get the straps more tangled.

"Hi, Lisa," Veronica greeted her over the stall door, walking toward her own horse's stall. Maybe Veronica could remind her what to do.

"Can you help me with this thing?" Lisa began. "I mean Carole showed me all about it on Saturday, but it's so complicated—"

"Sure," Veronica said agreeably. But instead of coming into the stall to help Lisa herself, she called down the stable's hallway, "Oh, Red! The new girl here,

Lisa, needs some help. Can you saddle Pepper for her?"

A man, perhaps twenty, emerged from a stall at the end of the hall. He had a pitchfork in his hand. He'd obviously been cleaning out one of the stalls. He didn't say anything to Veronica—he just glared at her. But he also nodded and put down his pitchfork. As soon as he began walking toward Lisa, Veronica continued into Cobalt's stall.

Lisa watched carefully as the guy—who introduced himself as Red O'Malley—put the tack on Pepper. It seemed so easy when he did it.

"If I'd have had to do this myself, class would be over by the time I'd be done," Lisa joked.

Red glanced at her. "You want to learn?" he asked, almost surprised.

"Well, sure," she said. "Isn't that what we're here to do?"

"I guess so," he said. He began to explain the parts of the bridle and the saddle to her, showing her how to put them on and fasten them securely. She'd heard it before, but she knew she'd have to hear it all several times more before she could do it herself.

"Thanks," she said, honestly grateful to him, as he helped her bring Pepper to the ring.

"Good luck," he told her as he left for the stalls.

Lisa brushed the good-luck horseshoe with her hand and mounted Pepper.

"Well done," Max said, handing her a riding crop.

She glowed a little bit at Max's compliment, but tried not to show it. Sedately, she began walking Pepper around the ring while the other girls finished tacking up and mounting.

Riding Pepper felt both strange and familiar, but not unpleasant. Lisa felt secure at a walk. It was a comfortable pace. She'd learned how to make her horse turn to the right or left; by moving the right or left rein away from the horse's neck you could turn his head in the direction you wanted to go. It surprised her a little when the horse, who, after all, had so much experience, followed her directions; she was so new at riding. But he did. If she held her hands still and sat down in the saddle with her back straight, he stopped. If she applied gentle pressure with her calves, he started again. Pepper did what she told him to do. It really worked! The horse was actually following her instructions. Lisa smiled to herself. She was riding.

CAROLE TIGHTENED DELILAH'S girth and led her to the mounting area. "I've got a job!" Stevie called to her, her eyes dancing with excitement. She was already in the ring, circling at a walk on Comanche.

Carole breathed a sigh of relief. If Stevie had a job, that meant she really might be able to earn the money to go on the trip. Maybe, just maybe, it would work out.

"What's the job?" Carole asked while she slipped her foot into the stirrup and lifted herself up.

"It's for one of my neighbors," Stevie said. "He's had a drainage problem with his gutters. He's asked me to clean them for him."

Stevie cleaning gutters?

Carole swung her right leg over the saddle and sat down on Delilah. She checked her stirrup length, and when she was satisfied it was correct, she pressed on the horse's sides with her legs and Delilah moved forward.

As soon as she could feel the horse's movement under her, Carole was transported. She was doing something she loved doing, but it wasn't just that. When she was on a horse, she was in a world where *she* was in control. Carole couldn't control Stevie any more than she could control her father—or than she could have controlled her mother's illness—but she could control Delilah. It was something they enjoyed together. And while she was riding, she didn't have to think of the funny picture of her friend Stevie cleaning gutters. Stevie probably didn't even know where the gutters were on a house!

Then class began.

"OKAY NOW, PAIR up!" Max called for the girls to ride in twos for their final rounds in the ring that day. Lisa had been concentrating so hard in class that she was nearly exhausted, but there *was* something wonderful about it.

"Oh, good!" Veronica said with delight in her

voice. "I'm your partner." She urged her horse up toward Lisa's and their horses trotted together. Lisa was having trouble keeping her horse at a steady trot. Pepper kept wanting to walk.

"Here's how you do it," Veronica said. "You tap him just behind your leg with your whip. It's what I do with Cobalt. It makes him keep going."

Lisa didn't like the idea of using a whip on Pepper, but Max had assured her that it didn't hurt the horse. He told her that a whip should be used to reinforce an instruction the horse already knew he was supposed to follow. Lisa tapped Pepper with the whip. He began trotting at the same pace as Cobalt.

Veronica leaned over toward Lisa while they trotted together. "Isn't some of this stuff just so boring?" Veronica asked.

To Lisa the class was hard, confusing, uncomfortable, difficult, and a little frightening. It wasn't boring at all. But it was lonely. She wanted to make friends at the stable. She liked Carole; she'd like to be her friend, but then she'd have to be Stevie's friend, too, and it wasn't likely Stevie would ever want to be hers. It seemed that the only person at the whole stable who wanted to talk to her was Veronica, the very girl her mother wanted her to become friends with. It was very tempting just to agree with Veronica. She was about to when Max spoke sharply to them.

"You girls can chatter all you want while you're having your sodas. Lisa, perhaps you don't know it, but our rule is that there is no talking during class."

Lisa felt her face flush.

"I'm the one who was talking, Max," Veronica volunteered.

Max's lips formed a thin line, but he said nothing to Veronica. He just continued with his instructions to the class. "Now, we'll finish our exercise for today with figure eights. Carole, you and Polly please lead off across the ring. . . ."

When the class was over Lisa just wanted to remove Pepper's tack and go home. She didn't want to talk with anybody over sodas in the tack room. She hoped her mother was waiting outside so she could go right home and escape to her homework.

"Here's your soda, Lisa," Veronica said, handing it to her. "Meg got the soda whip, but I thought you'd like to have yours right away. You looked thirsty to me."

"Thanks," Lisa said automatically, accepting the cold can. She took a drink. It did taste good to her. "And thanks, too, for telling Max you were talking. How come he didn't get mad? I thought he was all set to blow up at me."

"Oh, there are ways to manage Max," Veronica said airily. "Say, would you like to come to my house on Saturday after class? Maybe stay for dinner? I can talk my mother into letting us order a pizza—with *everything.*"

"Uh, sure," Lisa answered automatically. At least she was making a friend—one her mother would approve of—even if it wasn't the one she wanted. Then she realized that by agreeing to go to Veronica's after class on Saturday, she was agreeing to go to another class. Her mother would like that, too. Deep down, she wondered how *she* felt about becoming friends with Veronica, the girl who "managed" Max and ordered the stable boy around. But maybe a friend like that was better than no friend at all. Maybe.

CAROLE TOOK HER time untacking Delilah. She'd been hoping to have time to visit with Stevie, but Stevie had dashed out, spilling her soda as she went, as soon as she'd untacked her horse. Carole had to wait for her dad and he'd be at least another half-hour. She decided to groom Delilah, who was stalled next to Pepper.

Carole didn't mean to overhear the conversation between Lisa and Veronica, but the walls were only boards and there was open space at the top.

To Carole, Veronica was the most stuck-up person she'd ever known. And she liked to collect admirers. It sounded like Lisa was being recruited for the collection. That was too bad, too, because Carole thought Lisa was nice as well as smart. Maybe, Carole thought, if she hadn't been so busy with the horses and if Stevie hadn't been so busy with her jobs, they would have invited Lisa to TD's with them. That would have been nice. But it was too late for that now.

Carole picked up the brush and began working from the top of Delilah's neck, brushing vigorously. The last thing she heard was Veronica' whiny voice. "Tell your mother you're coming to my house and you'll be home about, oh, ten o'clock on Saturday."

That meant that from the end of class until it was time to go home, Lisa would be with Veronica for almost seven hours. Carole was glad she wasn't the one who was going to Veronica's. She wouldn't want to spend that much time with Veronica—ever!

LISA FELT REALLY good right after class on Saturday. Max had worked with her a lot during class. At first, it seemed like he was picking on her, but then, as she listened to him, she realized that he was trying to help her—and that if she listened to him, it would work.

They were working on a posting trot. Lisa had to rise and sit with the beat of the horse's hooves. Two things about it were difficult. The first was sensing the beat. The second was keeping her balance. But Max was patient and she was learning. Even Patch, whom she was riding again today, seemed to have patience with her.

"He's in a better mood today than when I rode him before," she said to Max.

"Why do you say that?" he asked.

"Because he's easier to ride today."

"Maybe," was all that Max said. "Okay, now up, down, up, down, up, down . . ."

Lisa tried her hardest to follow his instructions, and by the end of the lesson, she actually thought she had a good idea of what she needed to do.

"Now, instead of standing straight up, swing your hips forward and up—yes! That's it! Very *good*, Lisa. Nice job!"

Lisa could hardly believe it. She'd gotten a real compliment from Max. She had enjoyed the lesson and—although she hated to admit it to herself—she was really having fun riding. Another nice thing that happened was that Max kept telling Stevie to keep her mind on her riding. Lisa was still smarting from Stevie's trick. They hadn't spoken to each other since the first lesson. That was okay with Lisa.

Not only were all these nice things happening, but Lisa was making friends, too. Or at least one. This was the day she would go to Veronica's house.

Her mother had been somewhat horrified by the idea of Lisa returning home as late as ten o'clock, but when Lisa reminded her she'd be at *Veronica's*, Mrs. Atwood agreed.

As soon as class was over, however, things began going a little sour for Lisa. And then they went straight downhill from there. While she was still untacking Patch in his stall, Veronica appeared.

"Aren't you done *yet*? I don't want to keep my mother waiting," Veronica told her. Lisa squirmed at the idea of keeping Mrs. diAngelo waiting. She tried to hurry, but the more she tried, the more trouble she had with the tack.

"I've got the bridle all tangled and I can't loosen the girth," she complained.

"Here, I'll help you," Veronica said, sighing. She finished the job quickly, though she made it clear she wasn't happy about having to do Lisa's work for her. Then, as they carried the tack back to the tack room, Polly Giacomin came up to Veronica. She barely seemed to notice that Lisa was standing next to Veronica.

"Uh, hi, Veronica," she said. "My birthday's this week and I'm going to have a party. A magician is coming, too. Would you like to come?"

Lisa thought it was rude of Polly to invite Veronica to a party right in front of her, even if they weren't friends. After all, what were telephones for? But before she had a chance to feel really hurt, Veronica raised one eyebrow and stared at Polly with a blank look of surprise. "I'm busy," she told her.

"It's Friday afternoon," Polly said, apparently realizing too late that Veronica meant she'd be busy *whenever* Polly had a party. Polly looked down at the ground as her face turned red in embarrassment. She turned and walked away.

"Imagine that," Veronica said to Lisa. "Polly Giacomin thinks I'd go to her party. A *magician!*" She laughed out loud. "Polly probably expects her friends to wear paper hats, too! Is she for real?"

Lisa stared at Veronica uncertainly. She loved to see magic shows. A birthday party with a magician seemed pretty neat to her. Lisa couldn't figure out why Veronica objected to a magic show, but she had the distinct impression that arguing about it—or even asking about it—wouldn't help her friendship with Veronica in the least. She laid the saddle on its rack in the tack room and put the bridle on the bracket. "Come on, let's go meet your mother," she said.

Veronica looked out the window toward the parking area. "I don't think she's here yet," she said.

Lisa decided not to remind Veronica that she'd been rushing her for her mother's sake only a few minutes ago. Right then it seemed to her that about the worst thing that could happen would be if Veronica were to give *her* the same glare she'd given Polly Giacomin. Lisa kept quiet.

Mrs. diAngelo came to pick the girls up twenty minutes late. She was driving a Mercedes, and there were two large dogs in the back seat, tracking mud on the leather upholstery. Veronica jumped in the front seat, leaving Lisa to sit in the rear with the dogs. Lisa liked dogs okay, but these Labrador retrievers didn't seem to like her. They certainly weren't being very friendly. She spent the entire trip to Veronica's house trying to get enough space on the seat to sit. Neither Veronica nor her mother paid any attention to her problem. They were locked in battle in the front seat on the subject of a new pair of breeches for Veronica.

"Did you see *hers*, Mom?" Veronica said, pointing to Lisa in the rear. Mrs. diAngelo looked at Lisa in the mirror. "That's the kind I want—only in hunter green."

"Those won't suit you at all," Mrs. diAngelo said firmly. As she went on to describe exactly what was wrong with Lisa's riding pants, Lisa squirmed. She couldn't wait until the ride was over. By the time they arrived at the diAngelo house, Veronica and her mother weren't speaking to each other. But Lisa suspected Veronica would wear her mother down eventually.

Lisa couldn't imagine arguing with her mother until she wore her down. And she didn't think she'd like to have a mother who could be worn down like that. Even more important, she couldn't imagine taking up an argument with her mother in front of a guest.

The diAngelo house was grander than anything Lisa had ever seen, except in movies or on guided tours. It was a big old white colonial house, with a two-story portico in the front. The center of the house was three stories high. The wings were each two stories. The whole house was surrounded by perfectly trimmed bushes and glorious shade trees carefully spaced in the acres of lush grass, all set against a background of rolling Virginia hills. Behind the house, Lisa spotted a swimming pool, a garden shed that was larger than most garages she'd seen, and a guest house as big as her own home.

She swallowed deeply and closed her eyes to see if the house would disappear. When she opened them, the house was still there and Veronica was staring at her.

"Come on, Lisa. We don't have all day."

The dogs tumbled out of the car in front of Lisa, running into the beautiful house with their muddy feet. The girls followed them in.

The rest of the day was mostly a blur to Lisa. She had lived all her life in nice middle-class neighborhoods and nice middle-class homes. Veronica had apparently spent her life living in a palace. Lisa had a lot to learn about living in luxury, but Veronica knew it all. She knew how to get the maid to deliver a snack to their room. She knew how to get the gardener to vacuum three leaves off the bottom of the pool before they swam. She knew how to get the chauffeur to go for the pizza even after her mother had said the girls would eat whatever the cook made that night.

Lisa shook her head in amazement. No wonder Veronica had known how to order Red O'Malley to saddle Pepper for her. And actually, come to think of it, she seemed to have a good idea of how to order Lisa around. She never asked Lisa what they would do next. She *told* her. Lisa didn't mind too much because most of it was new to her, but there was a part of it that made her uncomfortable.

After they'd finished their pizza, Veronica made another announcement.

"Mom stopped at the shopping center to pick up a prescription before riding class and I snuck into Sights 'n' Sounds and rented this neat horror movie she wouldn't let me see. We'll watch it now." Veronica slipped the tape into the VCR in her room, which was connected up to her television.

Lisa looked at Veronica's clock radio and saw that it was eight-thirty. If she watched the movie, she'd never be able to be home by ten. Besides that, she didn't want to watch a horror movie, whether Mrs. diAngelo permitted it or not.

"I think it's time for me to go home," Lisa said.

"Home!" Veronica said, as if the very idea were a personal insult to her.

"Well, it's getting late, and I don't want Mom to have to come out after ten. She'd be annoyed, you know?"

"Don't be ridiculous!" Veronica said. "Your mother doesn't have to come here. We can have the chauffeur drive you home. It's no trouble at all."

Though Lisa wasn't crazy about the idea of a chauffeur driving her, it would solve one problem. She knew that if her mother had a chance of being invited into the diAngelo house, she'd want the grand tour of absolutely every inch of the mansion.

Veronica pushed the start button on her remote control, piling the pillows from her sofa on the floor to watch the movie in comfort.

"I think I'd better go home now," Lisa said firmly. Veronica gave her a dark look. Lisa felt cornered. "That pizza was a bit much, you know. I think it was the sausage. My stomach feels a little funny."

"I'll have the chauffeur get the car now," Veronica said, reaching for the intercom on her telephone.

CAROLE CARRIED A large bowl of fluffy, salty, buttery popcorn into the living room with one hand. The other hand held two cans of soda, precariously balanced, and two napkins.

"Ten hut!" she said sternly.

Her father, who had been stretched out on the sofa, jumped to attention. "I knew I smelled something wonderful," he told her, helping her unload the sodas.

"Well, it's quarter of nine and I know that *Casablanca* is on at nine. It's no fun watching a movie without buttered popcorn—and since *you* made dinner, I thought it was my turn for popcorn."

"There's still a front-row seat available, too," Colonel Hanson said, pulling a lounge chair up near the sofa, which he'd claimed for himself. Carole slid a small table between them and put the bowl on it. She had just settled into her seat when the phone rang.

"I'll get it, honey," said the colonel. "I want to get the salt anyway."

"Okay," Carole agreed, digging into the popcorn, which was salty enough for her taste.

Carole didn't know who was on the phone, but her father was chatting so agreeably that she suspected it was Stevie. The first time the two of them had met, they'd discovered their mutual passion for old jokes. Some of them were pretty corny but Stevie and Colonel Hanson seemed to love them.

Carole heard her father roar with laughter. "That's a good one. I'd forgotten that!" he said.

Carole stood up and walked into the kitchen, where her father was talking on the wall phone.

"Come on, Dad. Let *me* talk to Stevie."

"My daughter is pushing me around again, Stevie," he joked into the phone. "Next time we talk, though, I'm going to tell you the one about the gorilla on the golf course. Can't wait, can you?" he said before relinquishing the phone to Carole.

"Hi," Carole said. "What's up?"

"Oh, I'm just exhausted," Stevie said matter-of-factly. "I spent the whole afternoon after riding class going from door to door in my neighborhood, giving everybody fliers I had copied so they could tell me if they have work for me to do. Nobody did. They all just wanted to invite me in for cookies. Remind me next time not to accept cookies from Mrs. Crocker. She makes these health-food things and they're disgusting."

Carole laughed. Stevie then told her about the dogs who had chased her and about some people who were really rude to her. She told about one house that smelled funny and it turned out they were just putting up new wallpaper and did Carole know how funny new wallpaper smelled? She told Carole everything that had gone on. But there was one thing that hadn't gone on at all. Nobody had asked her to do any work.

"No luck, huh?" Carole asked.

"Oh, they'll call me eventually," Stevie assured her.

"But will 'eventually' be soon enough for the MTO?"

"Of course it will," Stevie snapped.

Stevie's moodiness was sometimes more than Carole could take. "What makes you think that?" Carole shot back. And then, wary of Stevie's fiery temper, she spoke quietly. "You know, you've really got me worried," Carole said. "The MTO is just two weeks from now and you're going to have a hard time earning so much money so quickly. I mean, what kind of jobs have you been offered so far? Cleaning pools, cleaning gutters? You can't do those things, can you?"

"No way," Stevie said. "I ended up giving both of those jobs to my brothers."

"But Stevie—" Carole began.

"Don't worry about me, Carole," Stevie said. She said it with such assurance that Carole was tempted to believe her. Did Stevie have something up her sleeve?

"To tell you the truth, I think it's *me* I'm worried about," Carole confessed. "I really hate the idea of going on that trip without you. Can you actually imagine me and Veronica and maybe that new girl, Lisa, on the camp-out? I'll spend the entire three days telling Veronica to take care of Cobalt herself."

"But you won't let her, will you?"

"No, of course I won't. She hasn't got the first idea of how to take care of that beautiful horse of hers. Cobalt would be better off living in the wild than with Veronica."

"Why don't you talk her into letting him run free and then you can capture him and own him yourself," Stevie suggested.

"*That's* the most sensible thing you've said tonight. And it doesn't make any sense either," Carole teased.

"Thanks, pal. I'm going to sit here now and wait for my customers to swamp me with calls. You go watch that movie with your father. Oh, and ask him for me: What's handsome and purple and says 'Play it again, Sam'? Bye!"

Carole hung up the phone and returned to the living room, where the movie was just beginning. Carole asked her father the riddle. He chuckled.

"What's the answer?" she asked him.

"Humphrey Bogrape," he told her.

Carole laughed, but it didn't make her feel any better about Stevie's chances of earning enough money.

"ARE YOU THE young boy who is looking for chores to do?" the voice on the phone asked. The phone had rung right after Stevie had hung up with Carole.

"Yes," Stevie answered. She didn't want to disagree with a potential customer.

"Well, the beds under my hedges need cleaning. Can you rake them out for me?"

Gardening work like that was hot, sweaty, and unpleasant. Stevie didn't even like to rake leaves in the cool weather in the fall.

"I'll pay two-fifty an hour," the woman continued.

"Sure," Stevie said eagerly.

"Monday at four o'clock?"

"I'll be there," she promised. She took the woman's name and address and then hung up.

Raking out from under hedges was not only difficult, but was a job for a small person who could crouch easily to reach the hard places—a younger person, perhaps one who was trying to save up money for a fifty-gallon fish tank. Someone just like her younger brother.

"Michael!" Stevie called upstairs.

Her nine-year-old brother appeared on the landing. "Yeah?" he asked suspiciously.

"Want to make some money?"

Michael smiled broadly, nodding.

The phone rang again. "Is this Stevie Lake?" a man asked when she answered. "I need someone to help me clean out my attic," he began. Stevie knew it was a perfect job for her twin brother, Alex.

Stevie made the arrangements and gave Alex all the information. By the time she'd finished with that, the phone rang again. She couldn't believe it. She had begun to think that walking around the neighborhood had been a dumb waste of time, but it seemed that a lot of people had work they wanted done. Stevie was nearly ecstatic.

The phone kept ringing all day Sunday, too. One woman wanted somebody to dig worms for her six-year-old son to use for fishing. Another needed somebody to till her vegetable patch for planting. Mrs. Ziegler wanted somebody to sit for the twins Wednesday afternoon. It seemed that everybody in the world had something they didn't want to do themselves. Stevie could understand that. After all, she didn't want to do her math project.

On Sunday night, practically exhausted from making plans on the telephone all day long, she fell into bed and closed her eyes. In her dreams, Stevie was riding Comanche proudly along the wooded trail, sleeping bag fastened to the back of the saddle. Only Stevie, Carole, and Max were on the trail, though. Everybody else was back in town: They were an army of kids doing loads and loads of chores for Stevie's neighbors. Stevie smiled contentedly in her sleep.

THERE WAS NO riding class on Monday, but Carole had called Veronica on Sunday to remind her that she'd promised Carole she could exercise Cobalt after school. Veronica had forgotten completely. Carole wasn't surprised. It wasn't so much the promise to Carole she'd forgotten; it was Cobalt who had slipped her mind again. But she readily agreed that Carole could do the job. Carole had the school bus drop her off by the shopping center and she got to Pine Hollow by three-thirty.

The outdoor ring was empty, so she'd be able to work with the beautiful Thoroughbred in the large exercise area. Smiling to herself, she entered his stall. He nickered and nuzzled her shoulder when she put her arm around his shiny, silky black neck.

"Poor old boy," she whispered into Cobalt's ear.

"Your problem is that you're too pretty. If you weren't so good-looking, Mr. diAngelo would never have bought you and you'd never belong to Veronica. You'd belong to somebody who would really care about you."

Not that Veronica didn't care about Cobalt, exactly. She cared about him in the same way she cared about her friends. They were part of a collection to her, things that made her feel more important just because they were hers.

Cobalt was a Thoroughbred stallion. Mr. diAngelo had paid a lot of money for him. But Cobalt wasn't the right kind of horse for Veronica. His personality didn't mesh with hers at all, though Carole wondered briefly if anybody's personality could mesh with Veronica's. Cobalt was high-strung and powerful. Veronica needed a horse she could control, and she couldn't control him. She was constantly fighting with him. Carole knew that it couldn't be much more fun for Veronica than it was for Cobalt, but she felt sorrier for Cobalt than she did for Veronica.

She slipped on his saddle and bridle and within a few minutes had led him out into the ring. Max was there training a new bay, which he had just bought as a school horse. He smiled broadly when he saw Carole and Cobalt.

"I always like to see you riding that horse, you know," he said.

"And I always like to ride him," Carole said. "I keep hoping that if I can ride him enough, he'll develop some confidence in people."

Max shook his head a little sadly. "He's a fine horse, and always will be. Veronica can't change that. But she can damage him as a riding horse. I mean, look at this one I'm on, Diablo. He was named that because of his short pointy ears." Carole looked at the ears and laughed. They did look a little devilish. "Anyway, this is a nice horse and he's gentle enough for most of the new riders. But his mouth is a little tough."

Carole knew what that meant. If a horse needed very strong signals with a bit to follow commands, he had a tough mouth. If a slight signal was followed, the horse had a soft mouth.

"Cobalt has a soft mouth. Every time I see Veronica tug at her reins, or ride on them, yanking away, I think about that soft mouth and how much it must hurt."

"No wonder he's so jumpy when Veronica's riding him," Carole said.

"But not with you," Max assured her.

Carole knew that was true and she was proud of it. Cobalt responded to the slightest pressure with the reins. In fact, he usually responded just to the pressure of her legs on his sides. Sometimes, it seemed to Carole that Cobalt could practically read her mind.

"Let's see how smart you and that horse really are,"

Max challenged her. "It'll give me a chance to test Diablo, too. I'll lead you on a figure around the ring. See if you can follow it."

Carole loved challenges like that. She was sure Cobalt would be up to it, too. Most riding classes were for the students. With a lot of work, and cooperation from the horses they rode, they could learn the basics of riding, and most students were perfectly content with that. Once the rider was schooled, however, the rider's goal became teaching the horses good manners and good form. This was known as dressage. In dressage competitions, it was the horse as much as the rider who was judged.

Max wanted to test Diablo and he wanted to give Carole a chance to have Cobalt show off his stuff. As a Thoroughbred, he was fast. Thoroughbreds were bred for racing. But Carole knew that Cobalt was smart, too, and she was eager for the challenge.

Max led off. He cantered Diablo down the center of the ring, turning him left at the corner. Then he began a figure eight crossing in the center of the ring. As he passed the center of the X, he changed leads, meaning that Diablo's gait switched from one lead leg to the other when he switched directions. A horse always had to lead with his inside leg on a circle, since all his weight was being thrown in that direction as he leaned into the turn. When the circle changed directions, as in a figure eight, the lead went from one side to the other.

With Max on board, the transition was smooth, barely noticeable. Max brought Diablo down to a walk and took him over to the side of the ring, making room for Carole.

With nearly invisible leg signals from Carole, Cobalt sprang into a balanced canter down the center of the ring. Carole swung Cobalt to the left and began her figure eight. As if he'd known all his life how to do it, Cobalt switched leads at the X both times they went through it.

"Beautiful, Carole, beautiful," Max said.

Carole knew it wasn't she who deserved the compliment. It was Cobalt.

Max worked with Carole and Cobalt for more than an hour, teaching both of them good habits and good manners. Never once did Cobalt try to take the bit or get fussy. He seemed as content to follow Carole's instructions as Carole was to give them.

"That's all for today," Max said. "You two have put in a lot of hard work. Time for a cooldown for both of you and a nice grooming—for Cobalt, that is!"

Carole dismounted and walked Cobalt in circles around the ring until he was cool enough for his grooming. She took him back to his stall and removed his tack. Then she brought the grooming tools back from the tack room.

Grooming a horse took a long time, but Carole didn't mind. When she groomed Cobalt, she thought he was the most beautiful horse in the world. She cross-tied him in his stall and began the job by cleaning out his hooves with a hoof pick. Next, she worked with a currycomb and then a brush all over his body, brushing out dust and sweat. She also used a comb and brush on his mane and tail. Then she used a damp sponge to smooth his coat and make it shiny. Finally, she put a blanket on him to protect his coat and to keep him warm in the cool spring evening that was coming.

When she was all done with that, she took a sugar lump from her pocket and gave it to him. Usually, Carole didn't like to give horses treats. They were better off eating their regular meals, and besides, a horse that got treats often began to expect treats all the time. Carole had seen horses who just wanted treats and would nip at their riders. It was a very bad habit horses developed sometimes.

But with Cobalt, it was different. He seldom got treats from Veronica, so he didn't expect them. He liked the sugar lumps Carole gave him, and the carrots she sometimes brought, but he always kept his good manners—at least with her. Veronica, however, often complained about how naughty he could be. Carole didn't think Cobalt was the one who was misbehaving at those times.

She gave Cobalt one final hug and left Pine Hollow to catch the bus for home at the shopping center.

When she owned her own stable some day, Carole decided, she wouldn't let in any owners who didn't take really good care of their horses, no matter how important the people thought they were.

"OH, IS *THIS* your house?" Veronica asked on Saturday afternoon as Lisa's mother drove them up the short driveway. Suddenly, Lisa was sure it was going to be a very long day.

The two girls retreated to Lisa's room. Mrs. Atwood said something about bringing milk and homemade marshmallow krispies in a few minutes. Lisa was glad her mother didn't see Veronica grimace.

Lisa liked her bedroom and she always had. It suited her very well. The walls were papered in pink flowers on a white background. She had a pink-and-white lounge chair covered in a fabric that matched the bedspread on her four-poster bed. She had a well-loved collection of stuffed animals by her pillow. On the far wall, next to her closet, was a small vanity with a large mirror. On the wall near the windows was the desk where she did her homework. There were two bookshelves containing her favorite books and some games and toys. There was a small rag rug near the bed. The rest of the floor was covered with wide wooden boards, which gleamed in the sunshine that streamed in every morning. As far as Lisa was concerned, it had everything she needed.

But she could see right away that for Veronica's taste it was missing a few things. There was no bedside telephone. No sofa. No television. No VCR. No stereo tape deck. No intercom to call the servants.

Veronica claimed the lounge chair. Lisa lay down on her stomach on her bed, facing Veronica. "I don't have a lot of the things you do," Lisa began apologetically.

"Where'd you get your breeches?" Veronica asked, ignoring Lisa's apology. Apparently, she and her mother were still arguing about riding pants.

"Mom and I went shopping at The Saddlery," Lisa said.

"Oh," Veronica said. It was just a sound like any other sound, but the way Veronica said it, it meant more than *oh.* It meant that Veronica bought her riding clothes at the fancier riding store at the West End Mall. It meant that even though Veronica had admired Lisa's pants, she wouldn't get a pair like them *because* they came from the less exclusive shop. Did it also mean that Veronica didn't really want to be friends with somebody who had to shop at The Saddlery?

Lisa began wondering about the type of girl who would make judgments about her friends based on where they bought their riding clothes. Just then, Mrs. Atwood came in with the milk and cookies. That time, Lisa knew her mother saw Veronica's grimace.

It was going to be a very long afternoon.

"STEVIE, ARE YOU working on your homework?" her mother called up the stairs.

Stevie didn't like to lie, but she didn't want to say no. She hated the idea of her mother coming into her room for a lecture right then. She compromised. "What else is a Saturday afternoon for?" she yelled, as if that were an answer. Her mother stayed downstairs.

Besides, in a way, she was working on her homework—her math project "substitute." All three of her brothers were in her room—and in on the conspiracy.

"Chad," she began, starting with her older brother. Chad was fourteen and very interested in girls. The only way she could get him to take any of the jobs she'd been flooded with was to promise that there were cute girls on the premises. "There's a lady on Granite Street who needs her grass cut this afternoon. Her name's Richman. I think she's Janet's mother."

"Oh, yeah, Janet," he said somewhat dreamily. "I'll do it."

"I knew you would," Stevie said, chuckling. "Alex, you want a dog-walking job?"

"As long as it's not a toy poodle or some other sissy kind of dog."

"I don't know what kind of dog it is. Just do it, will you?" she asked, a little annoyed. Quickly, her twin agreed.

"Michael, you did such a good job last week on those beds under the hedges that the lady wants you back for her flower beds."

"That lady kept calling me Stevie, you know, and I don't like to be called Stevie."

"Sure, she thinks I'm a boy. But she pays two-fifty an hour and that's two bucks clear for you." Stevie was very good at matching needs and skills—or greeds and skills, she thought to herself, laughing.

"I'll take it," Michael agreed.

"Okay, then, what are you all waiting for?" Stevie asked her brothers. "Go on, do your work."

They shuffled out of her room, but she barely saw them go. She had to make notes on her pad about which jobs had been filled and who was doing them. Just as she finished, the phone rang again.

"Stevie," a girl whined. "It's Polly. I can't do that baby-sitting job on Wednesday. I have an orthodontist appointment—"

"I'll call Mrs. Ziegler and see if it's okay for you to

take the twins to your orthodontist," Stevie said, thinking fast.

"No way!" Polly said. "They're little monsters! They'd probably kill the fish in Dr. Mellman's fish tank. Get somebody else."

"Okay," Stevie agreed and then hung up. But *who*? She decided to try the new girl in her riding class. After all, she lived pretty near the Zieglers. Maybe that meant she knew how awful the twins were, Stevie thought, pausing while she reached for the phone. Before she could make up her mind, the phone rang again.

"Is this Stevie? Would you like a job helping me take all the stuff out of my basement? It flooded in those rains last week and everything needs to be dried, you see . . ."

"YOU JUST WOULDN'T believe all the calls I'm getting," Stevie told Carole on the phone later that night. "I mean, my ear is sore—"

"Stevie, just exactly what *did* you put on that flier you handed out?" Carole asked. Their town was full of kids who wanted jobs to do, and she couldn't understand why everybody was calling Stevie.

"Oh, I suppose it was kind of a hard sell," Stevie said vaguely. Whenever Stevie got vague, she was trying to cover something up.

"'Hard sell'?"

"Yeah, sort of."

"Like what, specifically?" Carole said.

"Want me to read it to you?" Stevie asked.

"Yes, I'm dying to know what you said," Carole shot back.

"Okay, here goes." Stevie sighed. "It says 'I'm desperate for money! Please hire me to do odd jobs for you. Nothing is too big or too small for me. I'll do any kind of honest work. I must have cash immediately to put a shelter over my head and food on my plate! Signed, A Starving Twelve-Year-Old. Call 555-7823 and ask for Stevie.'"

"Stevie, I don't believe you! Haven't you heard about truth-in-advertising laws?"

"Well, it's sort of true. I mean, I'm earning the money to pay for the tent and the food on the camping trip, aren't I? And it's working, isn't it? I mean, I've had dozens of calls—uh, say, would you groom Cobalt on Monday?"

"Well, sure, I'll always groom Cobalt, but—"

"Uh, thanks. Listen, Carole, I've got to go. See you," she said, and hung up before Carole could ask her why *she* was finding somebody to groom Cobalt. Carole decided that Stevie had agreed to do it for the Original Lazy Bones, Miss V. diAngelo, but had gotten a paying job for the same time. Well, if that were going to help Stevie be able to go on the trip, then Carole was glad to do it. Besides, she was always glad for a chance to groom Cobalt.

But Carole was still uneasy about her friend's project as she got ready to go to sleep.

LISA LAY BACK in bed, watching the half-moon in the clear sky outside her window. The moon was reflected in her vanity mirror—two half-moons a quarter of a million miles apart. If she could put them together, would she have a full moon? Perhaps the halves wouldn't match. These days, it seemed to her a lot of halves didn't match.

Even though she had thought she would hate riding, now that she was doing it, she loved it. She had been wrong about that half. She had thought she wouldn't ever be any good at it, but Max had praised her today. Max didn't lavish praise on anybody. She knew that she'd worked hard and deserved it.

She had thought that it would be fun to be Veronica diAngelo's friend. But being a friend to Veronica didn't mean having Veronica be a friend to her. Those were two halves that didn't match at all.

Lisa was beginning to realize—no, if she wanted to be honest with herself, she'd have to admit that the signs had been there ever since Veronica had summoned Red O'Malley to help her—that Veronica was a very selfish person. She may have been willing to share her VCR and her parents' chauffeur with Lisa, but she didn't seem to be able to share herself. She wasn't much of a friend, Lisa decided finally.

Riding was something you did with other people. Riding classes were for groups, not individuals. A horseback camp-out would be really neat—if she had a friend to share it with. But Veronica would have a hard time sharing that, too, Lisa knew. It would be horrible, just horrible, if she couldn't be friends with anybody at riding class, but that seemed to be the case. And if that were true, she'd have to give up riding. Her mother wouldn't mind now, not after she'd seen how rude Veronica could be—the "great" Veronica diAngelo. The *rich* Veronica diAngelo was more like it, since that seemed to be the single most important thing as far as Veronica was concerned.

Lisa closed her eyes for just a few minutes. When she opened them again, the moon had set. The sky was dark except for the soft sparkle of a few stars. The mirror on her vanity was completely dark.

LISA STOOD CAUTIOUSLY next to Pepper in his stall. It was Tuesday, time for her next riding class. She was still feeling torn about her riding lessons. It was one thing to have fun with horses, another to have fun with friends, and it didn't seem to her any more likely that the two things would happen together at Pine Hollow Stables than it had while she was trying to get to sleep on Saturday night. She was probably going to quit. She'd just about made up her mind when her mother had loaded her into the car to come to this lesson. Now she was sure. This would be her last.

She was uncomfortably aware of Veronica in Cobalt's stall next to Pepper's. Veronica was having a hard time with her Thoroughbred and, as Lisa listened, it seemed that the horse was having a hard time with his owner. There was a loud thump when Veronica swung the saddle onto Cobalt's back—and a second thump just as loud when the saddle hit the ground. Lisa knew that if you threw a saddle onto a horse's back, he was likely to object. And she couldn't say she blamed him!

"You dumb horse," Veronica whined. "I'll have to get Red to saddle you. Red! Where are you?" she called. There was no answer. Lisa had seen Red in the tack room and knew he could hear Veronica perfectly well. It didn't really surprise her that Red was ignoring Veronica's call. She decided to do the same.

Lisa smoothed the saddle pad onto Pepper's back and then gently swung the saddle up onto the dappled gray horse. He shifted his weight from one side to the other, but he remained standing still. Then, just as Red had showed her, she checked the pad for wrinkles and then lifted the saddle forward over the end of the mane so she could slide it back into place, brushing Pepper's coat in the right direction. She had learned that if she didn't do that, she'd end up with the saddle too far back and she'd be tilted forward when she tried to ride.

The front of the saddle had to be at the horse's withers. When she first heard the word, Lisa thought withers sounded like something shriveled, but Red had told her it was just the name for the slight bump in a horse's back at the top of his shoulders.

When she was sure the saddle was in the right place, she reached for the girth.

At that moment, Lisa heard Carole's voice. "You want some help?"

Lisa was about to say yes, then realized that Carole wasn't talking to her. She was talking to Veronica, who eagerly said yes.

"That stupid, lazy Red! He won't give me any help and I'm sure he's not taking proper care of my beautiful horse," Veronica said petulantly.

Carole didn't answer that. She began talking to Cobalt. "There, there, boy," she said soothingly. Lisa could hear her patting the horse's neck. He nickered gently in response. Carole continued talking to him while she tacked him up. There were no thumps and bumps this time. It was as if the horse understood her. When the bridle had been secured, Carole spoke to Veronica. Perhaps because she couldn't see her—only hear her—Lisa was particularly aware of the change in Carole's voice when she spoke to Veronica. The assurance was gone. The gentleness was missing. Carole, the totally assured Carole, was apparently uncomfortable talking to Veronica.

"I really had a good ride on Cobalt the other day. Max and I were working on things with him in the ring. I—"

"I hope you didn't tire him out, Carole," Veronica spoke sharply.

"No, I didn't. I just rode him for an hour for exercise, but I was wondering if I could—"

"Carole," Veronica spoke again, this time more sharply. Lisa was surprised that Carole could be spoken to this way, but Veronica seemed to have the upper hand. "You haven't . . . "

"Look, Veronica, don't talk to me like that. I didn't tell anybody, not even Max, that you slammed the door and scared Patch. If you want to add Lisa to your collection, it's okay with me, but I think she's too smart for you."

"Collection?" Veronica said, as if she didn't understand the word. "I'm sure Lisa's smart, but we really don't have anything in common. She's not even a good rider," Veronica said smugly.

"Good rider?" Carole echoed. Then, suddenly on the offensive, she challenged Veronica. "What would you know about that?"

There was a moment of silence before Veronica spoke again. "Listen, Carole, if you'd like to ride Cobalt again on Thursday, it's okay with me. Just don't get him too tired this time, okay?"

The next sound Lisa heard was the clunking of Cobalt's hooves as Veronica led him to the mounting block. Lisa ducked below the edge of the wooden wall of the stall so that neither girl would know she'd been there.

Her hands felt clammy. It was humiliating to hear herself discussed that way. An addition to a collection? Nothing in common? Not even a good rider? What was she? Some kind of toy to be played around with? Just who did Veronica diAngelo think she was? *She thinks she's the daughter of Willow Creek's richest resident, that's who she thinks she is,* Lisa answered her own question.

And then the tears came. Once they started, there seemed to be no way to stop them. She sniffled and tried to wipe them away and she stifled the cries she wanted to make. There was no way in the world she would ever, *ever* let that awful girl Veronica know she'd hurt her. No way!

"Pepper, you okay?" Carole's voice came toward the stall. "Say, what's up, boy? Your gear on okay? I'll check it for you," she said. And then the stall door slid open and Carole stepped in. There was no place for Lisa to hide from her. As soon as Carole saw her, she knew what had happened. The look on her face confirmed it.

"You heard that, huh?" Carole asked.

Lisa nodded.

"Better now than later," she said matter-of-factly. "Veronica's a rotten person. You shouldn't believe anything she ever says about anybody—good or bad."

Sitting on the straw in the stall, Lisa drew her legs up to her chest and put her forehead on her knees. The last few tears dropped onto the straw. When her crying stopped, she looked up at Carole, who had put on the bridle and was patting Pepper.

"What about *you*?" she asked. "When do *you* tell the truth?"

"Me?" Carole looked at her, puzzled.

"Yes, *you.* You knew all along that it was Veronica who slammed the door the day I was riding Patch, didn't you?"

"Well, yes, but—"

"But what? Why didn't you tell me?"

"What difference would it have made?" Carole asked.

"It would have kept me from thinking I could be her friend. I would have known right away that she was a jerk—"

"Everybody knows that," Carole said.

"Well, I didn't; I'm new. Anyway, it would have kept me from blaming Stevie," Lisa told her.

"You thought *Stevie* did that?" Carole asked, astonished. Lisa nodded. "Oh, boy," Carole shook her head. "Stevie does jokes, all right—like the dumb thing with your stirrups—but she'd never, and I mean *never*, do something dangerous like slamming a door when Patch was around." Carole paused. "I guess you deserve an explanation," she said. "The reason I didn't tell you it was Veronica was because if I had, she wouldn't have let me ride Cobalt. He's the most wonderful horse in the world, and I couldn't give him up. I'm really sorry if it hurt you, though."

Lisa stared at her, astonished. Before she could speak, though, the loudspeaker in the stable area crackled. "Time to assemble for class," Mrs. Reg's voice announced.

"Oh, no!" Carole squealed. "I have to tack up Delilah. Say, you want to go over to the shopping center after class, maybe get some ice cream at TD's?"

"Uh, sure," Lisa said uncertainly.

LISA WAS RELIEVED when class began. When she was trying to figure out how to tack up a horse or make sense out of her classmates, everything was a hopeless muddle. But when Max was running the class, it was very clear what she had to do. She had to do exactly what Max told her. And when she did what Max told her to do, Pepper did what she wanted him to do.

All the horses were lined up to trot around the outdoor ring when Stevie arrived.

"We're proud to have you join us, Miss Lake," Max said. Some of the girls giggled, but Lisa could tell from the tone of his voice that he wasn't being funny. He took riding very seriously and didn't like to have any disruptions in his class. A student coming in late was a disruption. So was talking. So was not paying attention. Max didn't seem to care if you didn't know things, or if you'd forgotten how to do something. The important thing was for you to try as hard as you could. If you were late, or talking, or not paying attention, you weren't trying.

"I'm sorry, Max. There was something I had to take care of and it made me late. I promise—"

"It won't happen again?"

"Yes, Max. It won't happen again," she said, and then mounted Comanche. She joined the end of the trotting line.

Max had them working at keeping the distance between their horses the same. Lisa found it very hard to do. Pepper liked to trot and he liked to trot quickly. He seemed to have a natural competitive spirit, always wanting to catch up to and pass the horse in front of him.

Lisa was riding behind Polly Giacomin. Her horse, Nero, was an old stable horse. He'd taken so many classes he knew the routines better than Max. In fact, he'd learned them the same way Max had. They'd both been trained by Max's father. Nero seemed to know exactly how slowly he could go and get away with it. Lisa was becoming exhausted trying to get Pepper to go more slowly, and wished Polly would get Nero going a little faster.

Usually, Max would have been after both of them, urging Polly to "trot on," and telling Lisa to control her horse. Both of them certainly deserved warnings today. But Max's attention was focused on Stevie.

"Stevie, use your legs to even your horse's pace. Stevie! Your diagonals! Come on, now, you missed the beginning of the class, you've got to catch up. I won't have you slacking off!"

Stevie just nodded. Lisa cringed a little bit for her, surprised to find herself feeling sorry for Stevie Lake.

Maybe she was more relieved that Max wasn't watching her so closely this time.

"Stevie Lake! There's a phone call for you," Mrs. Reg announced over the loudspeaker. "It seems to be very important. Please come to the office."

"Uh, Max, could I please be excused to go to the phone?" Stevie asked politely.

Max glowered in silence while Stevie led Comanche to the gate of the ring.

STEVIE WAS HAVING a horrible day. Two of the people she'd gotten jobs for this afternoon hadn't shown up. Right before she had left home, there had been the two furious phone calls. She'd only had time to make a few calls, looking for replacements, and ended up leaving a desperate note for Alex before she'd had to run over to Pine Hollow. And then she'd been late.

"Hello," she said warily into the phone.

"Stevie, it's Alex. I got the note and there is no way I'm going to go shopping with old Mrs. Ramsey. She's a crabby lady and —"

"Alex, I'm desperate!" Stevie wailed over the phone. "Sid Jackson said he'd do it and then he ratted out. Mrs. Ramsey just needs somebody to go along and help her read the labels and stuff and then carry things home for her."

"*No* way," Alex said.

"She's a poor old woman, can barely see; she just needs a helping hand for an hour or so."

"No way."

"I'll pay you the full five dollars," she said, her voice dripping with temptation.

There was silence for just a moment. Alex sighed and then spoke. "All right. Just this once. But never again!"

"You ungrateful—" Stevie began, but she didn't bother to finish. Alex had hung up on her.

Stevie hung up the phone and walked out of the office to return to class. She released the knot in Comanche's lead rope but then saw the horses trotting in pairs. Class was almost over. There was no point in going back to the ring. She led Comanche back to his stall for untacking, going over her checklist of the things she needed to do before she went home. She had to give Carole her money for grooming Cobalt yesterday, but first, she had to collect it from Veronica. Then, she had to stop by Mrs. Traeger's to get paid for the job one of her classmates had done there yesterday. Then she had to go and fill in on the sitting job for Mrs. Vitelli that Betsy Cavanaugh had begged out of and then she had to—

"Stevie!" It was Max. Stevie stiffened when she heard his tone of voice; he didn't sound happy. Normally, she liked talking to Max. He was a wonderful teacher and a good rider and a nice man. But he took riding seriously and Stevie knew that she had been pretty sloppy today.

"Stevie, can you spare me a minute?" he asked sharply.

"Yes, Max," she said.

"Then please come to the office when you've untacked Comanche."

"I'll be there in a second," she said, knowing that all the other things on her list would have to wait. After all, riding was very important to her. The only reason she was working was to be able to go on the MTO. Max would understand that, she told herself. Wouldn't he?

"You ready to go?" Carole asked, peering into Pepper's stall. When she saw Lisa hugging Pepper, she was glad she'd decided to be friendly. It had been tempting to ignore Lisa, with her fancy riding clothes, trying to be Veronica's friend. But something about the way Lisa was handling Pepper told Carole that although there was a lot Lisa didn't know about riding, there was little she wouldn't learn. They had a lot in common.

"Just a minute more," Lisa told her. "I just wanted to visit with Pepper a little."

"You had a good ride on him today, didn't you?" Carole asked. She'd noticed how well-behaved the horse had been in class, and it was obvious that Lisa was having fun riding him.

"Yeah. But you know, I don't understand something." Carole nodded, waiting. "The first time I rode him, he was sort of hard to handle. He didn't do anything I wanted him to. The next time, he was better, and every time since then, he's been better. Was he sick or something?"

Carole started laughing, but stopped when she saw that she was hurting Lisa's feelings. "I'm sorry," she said. "I'm not making fun of you, it's just that this almost always happens with new riders," she said. "They think they're getting better horses with every lesson, but what's actually happening is that their horses are getting better riders. You see, the more you know, the more you let the horse know who's in charge. A horse somehow senses when a rider doesn't know what she's doing. And horses will take advantage of that right away. That's why Max usually starts the newest riders on Patch. He's very gentle and sweet—"

"Except when he's frightened, right?"

"That's right. Normally, you could trust him with a two-year-old. But Pepper, on the other hand, has a mind of his own. You've just learned enough about riding to show Pepper you're the boss. You've learned a lot in just a few lessons, you know?"

Lisa's face flushed a little pink. She was both pleased and embarrassed. Carole was such a good rider that a compliment from her was almost as good as one from Max. She didn't know how to respond, so she changed the subject from riders to horses. "Are horses really that different from one another?" Lisa asked.

"You bet they are," Carole said. "As different as people are. Pepper's a nice even-tempered horse—as long as he knows what he's supposed to do. If his rider starts giving him confused signals, say kicking with the legs to go forward and pulling on the reins to stop, he'll get really stubborn. He likes things just so. Max really trusted you when he put you on Pepper."

Lisa gave the horse one final hug and pat, and when she was sure he was safe in his stall, she picked up the tack and stepped out into the hall. Carole rolled the door shut and latched it with the bolt and the key chain snap.

"What about Cobalt?" Lisa asked. "What's he like?"

"Cobalt's a high-strung Thoroughbred. His mother is a hunter-jumper and his father was a racehorse. In horse talk, that's his dam and his sire. Anyway, the result of breeding like that is that he's very competitive—always has to be at the front of the pack. He competes with horses *and* with people and he always wants to take charge. If his rider gives him his way, forget it, he's almost uncontrollable."

"Is that why Veronica has such a tough time with him?"

"Yeah, and she's scared of him, too."

"Would he hurt her?" Lisa asked.

"Probably not. Most horses never want to hurt people, but they're so big that sometimes they can't help it. Anyway, there's a greater danger that Cobalt would hurt himself than his rider if he got out of control." Carole hated the idea of an innocent horse being hurt by a thoughtless or careless rider. She was thoughtfully silent while she helped Lisa hang up Pepper's bridle. They each took the soda that Meg Durham gave them and left the stable, heading for the shopping center.

"Then there's a horse like Nero," Carole continued. "He's so laid-back that you think he's lazy. But really, he's just taking life at his own pace!"

"I know that. I was trying to hold Pepper's trot behind Nero today. It wasn't easy!"

"No, it wasn't. But you were doing a pretty good job," Carole told Lisa. "And Max noticed it, too."

"Hey, Carole, wait up!" Stevie called out. Carole stopped and turned around. Stevie was dashing after them.

"I thought you'd left already," Carole said, and then she remembered that Max had talked to Stevie after class in his office. "What did Max want?"

"Oh, he gave me the usual lecture about paying attention and how Pine Hollow was serious about developing riders and how he didn't want riders who weren't serious about learning. You know the stuff.

Anyway, I wanted to give you this." She held out her hand, offering four dollars to Carole.

"What's this for?" Carole asked.

"It's for Cobalt," Lisa said.

"So put it in his bank account—at the diAngelo Trust Company." Carole laughed at her own joke.

"No, it's not for the horse, Carole. It's for you—for grooming him yesterday."

"I groomed him because you asked me to, not for money," Carole said, a little annoyed that Stevie would think she'd have to pay her for a favor.

"Well, the reason I asked you to was because Veronica paid me to do it. So the money's for you," Stevie explained.

Carole looked at the money for a moment. "But you're the one who needs it for the MTO. You keep it."

"I did keep some of it—sort of my commission. Don't worry about me. I'll make it. You take this because you earned it. And I don't have time to argue now. Bye." She slammed the four dollars into Carole's hand and ran back up the stable's driveway, where her mother was waiting for her behind the wheel of their station wagon.

Carole shoved the money into her pocket. "You know, Lisa, I understand horses. They make sense to me. It's people who are confusing. Stevie wants to go on the MTO so badly, but she's doing absolutely everything wrong. First, all she had to do was a math project, but no, that wasn't good enough for Stevie. So then, she decided to earn money, but no, she's too good to do the work. I never saw anybody so eager to turn jobs over to other people. So then, while she isn't doing either of those things, she's busy getting Max so angry with her that he might not *let* her go on the trip. Some fix she's getting into."

"Listen, you tell me about horses, and I'll tell you about people," Lisa said.

"What do you mean?" Carole asked.

"I mean, Stevie isn't so dumb."

"What are you talking about?"

"Stevie just said she was taking commissions," Lisa said. "Look, how much money does Stevie need for the trip?"

"Fifty dollars," Carole said.

"Okay, well, she's been very busy, you know."

"Yeah, I know. She's been busy on the phone giving away all her money-earning opportunities. At the rate she's doing it, everybody in town *but* Stevie will be able to afford the trip."

"Oh, no wonder you're so worried about her! Stevie isn't giving work away, she's selling it! Don't you see, she's getting a commission on every job she lines up. Somehow, she's managed to get everyone in town to call her to do work. It's way more than she can do herself, so instead of doing it herself, she's a one-girl employment agency. See, she got you to curry Cobalt—"

"How come you know all this?" Carole asked.

"She told me about it when she called me to see if I could baby-sit for the Ziegler twins tomorrow, but I can't—"

"That's a good thing," Carole interrupted. "They are real monsters."

"See, you *do* understand people," Lisa teased, and then she and Carole laughed together. "Anyway, every time Stevie gets somebody to do a job, she takes a little bit of the money they earned. That's her commission for getting them the job. She gave you four dollars for grooming Cobalt, right?" Carole nodded, feeling the crumpled bills in her pocket. "Well, Veronica probably paid her five dollars. So you did the work, but she got a dollar."

"But that's just one dollar of fifty she needs. She could have earned *five*—"

"Right, but while you were doing that job for her, three other kids were probably doing other jobs for her. And she probably got a dollar for each of those jobs, too. Maybe more. She got to sit home and wait for the phone to ring while she earned four dollars."

And if she earned four dollars on one weekday afternoon, Carole thought, then she could certainly earn a lot more on Saturdays and Sundays. She'd be able to earn fifty dollars and go on the MTO if—and it seemed like a pretty big *if* today—Max would let her go.

"Don't worry, Carole. Stevie seems like a person who can figure out all the angles. She'll make it, I'm sure."

Carole wished she were so sure.

Carole and Lisa arrived at the shopping center and made their way past the supermarket to get to TD's.

"Guess what?" Carole asked.

"What?" Lisa said.

"This is going to be my treat because I just got four dollars I never expected to have."

"You don't have to pay for me," Lisa protested.

"Well, think of it as Stevie's treat, her way of making up for that stirrup trick your first day, okay?"

"Well, okay," Lisa said. "But then I'm going to have to find a way to make up for all those knots in her sneakers."

"You will," Carole told her. "You will." And she was sure it was true. She was glad she had invited Lisa to TD's today. She wished she'd done it sooner.

"TELL ME MORE about the horses at the stable," Lisa said to Carole. The two of them sat at a corner table inside TD's. The threat of rain had kept them from the picnic tables behind the shop. Their empty ice cream dishes sat in front of them as they chatted. For the first time since she'd started riding, Lisa was really happy about it. She was getting better at riding, but most important, she had a friend.

Carole sat across the table from her, talking animatedly about her favorite subject: horses. She smiled as she described the horses at Pine Hollow. "Well, then there's Comanche. He and Stevie are a perfect match—you know it's important to match up personalities, don't you? I mean, you can't have a flighty horse with a vague rider. A flighty horse needs to be told what to do all the time. Anyway, Comanche is very strong-willed. So is Stevie. And when they both want to do the same thing at the same time—wow!"

Lisa laughed. "And when they want to do different things?"

"Stevie's a good rider," Carole said. "Comanche follows her orders. Usually."

"You mean like when she was changing direction, and he didn't want to?" Lisa asked. Class always began with the horses going in a clockwise direction. Several times during the class, they switched to counterclockwise so that the horses didn't get too used to one direction or the other. Stevie was supposed to lead the class across the center of the oval ring to change direction. Comanche had wanted to keep on going clockwise. "I thought she'd just let him go around to the back of the line and let him follow the other horses. He'd have gone counterclockwise then, wouldn't he?"

"He probably would have," Carole agreed. "But then, he would have won the argument, and it's not a good idea to let a horse do that. So she kept turning him to the left until he finally went."

"It looked pretty silly," Lisa said.

"Sure it did, but he didn't misbehave through the rest of the class, did he?"

"No, he didn't. Horses are like little children, aren't they?"

Carole nodded. "Sometimes they can be pretty

bratty, too. But the rider can't let the horse be in charge."

"What do you like best about riding, Carole?"

Lisa watched Carole's face while she considered the answer. It seemed to take a long time. Lisa hadn't thought it was a difficult question.

"Everything," Carole said finally.

CAROLE SAT ON the bench at the bus stop. She had fifteen minutes until her bus arrived and not much to do until then. But she couldn't wander around. The last time she'd done that, she'd missed the bus and had to wait another half hour.

She didn't mind waiting, really. Sometimes she'd see friends, and if that didn't happen, she could look in the nearby store windows. She stood up to stretch her long legs and wandered over to the display window at Sights 'n' Sounds. She smiled, remembering the tape she'd bought for her father. He'd loved it. If she'd had enough money on her then, she would have bought another one.

There was a big sign in the window that read: GRAND PRIZE WINNERS. Something about that rang a bell. Then Carole remembered the contest that Stevie had entered while she was buying the tape for her father. Stevie had spun quite a fantasy about Hawaii, Carole remembered, smiling. Well, the winner had been announced now, and Stevie wasn't going to

Hawaii—at least not in *that* contest. Below the winner's name, there was a list of about twenty-five other people—second-, third-, fourth-, and fifth-prize winners and honorable mention. Something must have caught Carole's eye subconsciously because she leaned closer and peered at the small type. And right there, practically at the top of the list, was "Stevie Lake."

Carole looked again. Stevie's name really *was* there. It hadn't moved or changed. Stevie had actually won a prize. Her best friend was a winner! It took a few minutes to figure out what "Third Prize" next to Stevie's name meant: she'd won a portable cassette player. So, it wasn't a trip to Hawaii, or even a fifty-dollar cash award—which would have been perfect!—but it was a prize. Carole was so excited that she wanted to call Stevie right away.

She pulled some change out of her pocket and looked for a phone. There were phones at the shopping center, but she couldn't remember where they were. Finally, she spotted one near the supermarket. She dashed across the parking lot, barely noticing the cars. Her phone call was too important.

She dropped the change into the phone and dialed the number she knew by heart. Busy. She tried again. Same thing. To kill some time, she paced up and down in front of the supermarket. But when she had her back to the phone, a boy and a girl got into the booth to make a call. Carole tapped her foot restlessly, watching shoppers emerge from the supermarket. After the couple had made not one, but three calls, they came back out of the phone booth.

Carole picked up the phone and dialed Stevie's number again. It rang. And rang. And then, at the sixth ring, Carole spotted her bus coming into the shopping center. She slammed the phone down and ran for it.

But the bus stop was all the way across the parking lot from the telephone, and riding boots were not the best running shoes. She clunked along as fast as she could, but all Carole got for her trouble was a faceful of carbon monoxide from the rear of the receding bus.

Carole growled. Annoyed with herself, she returned to the telephone. This time, she got an answering machine, but it was the wrong number. She slammed the phone down, realizing that now she was out of change. She couldn't make another call.

She returned to the bench at the bus stop and promised herself she wouldn't move until the next bus came. She put her elbows on her knees and her chin in her cupped hands and glared at the world. The afternoon had been going so well, she thought, remembering the fun she'd had with Lisa. Why did it have to end this way?

"Hi, baby! I thought I might find you here." Her father's cheerful voice greeted her from the car that had pulled up at the bus stop. "I had an errand in town and was just hoping to see you after your riding class. I'll take you home."

One of the things Carole loved about her father was that he always seemed to be there when she needed him. She grinned happily and climbed into the front seat next to him.

"STEVIE! IT'S ANOTHER phone call for you—and if it's another woman who wants a dog named Fifi walked, get somebody else to do it!"

That's how grateful my brothers are, Stevie thought to herself in disgust. She'd been working hours every day to get them jobs so they could earn money, and all she got were complaints. She promised herself she'd get somebody *else* to do the next job. There were lots of people she could call. She just wasn't sure who they were.

Carefully, she laid aside the scraps of paper that had her notes on them. She was in the middle of transferring all the information to her notebook. She had so many customers and so many workers that she had to keep careful records about who owed her money and how much of that had to be paid to the workers. While it wasn't always clear to her how much was coming in and going out, she knew exactly how much was *staying* in. She knew what her portion of the earnings was. And the news was great. She had more than sixty-five dollars. She *would* go on the overnight camp-out after all!

When the scraps of paper were neatly piled on her desk, she stood up to answer the phone call. Maybe it would be another job. Who would she get to do it? Obviously, not her ungrateful brothers. Her mind raced as she headed for the phone. She still had a few friends left in her class, and she could borrow Chad's and Michael's class lists, too; even though she didn't know the kids, they'd probably be glad for work.

"Hello?" she said more positively than she felt. She didn't really like the idea of calling her brothers' classmates.

"Stevie, it's Carole. You won! I was at the mall next to Sights 'n' Sounds and they've got the winners in the window and you won. Remember the contest that you entered when we were there? Your name is in the window!" she finished breathlessly.

"Huh?" Stevie said blankly. She'd been so concerned with her next job that she almost hadn't recognized Carole's voice. What *was* she talking about? She didn't remember anything about a contest except—

"Hawaii? I'm going to *Hawaii?!*"

"Oh—no. Somebody else won that. But you won a portable cassette player," Carole said, rushing on. "I mean, your name's right there in the window. I've been trying to call you for hours, but your phone's been busy or else there wasn't any answer or . . . anyway, you have to go to the store to pick up your prize. Can you believe it?"

"You sure?"

"Sure I'm sure! You *won* something. Isn't that wonderful?"

Finally, it hit Stevie. "You mean I actually won something in that contest?"

"Uh-huh."

"Wow, thanks for calling. I can't believe it! That's great. I'll go over there right now and get it. Only problem is that I've got all my favorite albums on records. I don't have anything to play on a tape machine." Once Stevie's mind was focused on a problem, her concentration was total.

"Doesn't Alex have a tape deck? You could borrow some of his tapes."

"You think I want to listen to the junk he likes?"

"Well, maybe you could buy a tape for the machine," Carole suggested.

"Maybe," Stevie said vaguely. "Hey, I'd better go over there. This is fantastic. Thanks for calling, Car." She slid the phone into its cradle.

Stevie was almost shaking with excitement. She'd won a contest. She, Stevie Lake, who'd never even won a game of musical chairs at a birthday party, had now won something in a contest. She grinned so happily that her cheeks almost hurt. She couldn't believe it.

"I won a contest," she said out loud. The words sounded very strange to her. She sat on the edge of her bed and took three deep breaths. Was this really happening?

How could she be sure it was real if she didn't go over there right away to claim her prize? She had more than an hour until dinner. That would be plenty of time. Sights 'n' Sounds was a fifteen-minute walk.

She stood up to leave her room. She'd need identification, she knew. She took her wallet. It had her library card in it as well as all her saved-up money. When she was sure she had everything she needed, she left her room and practically flew down the stairs and out the door.

"I won a contest!" she repeated to herself, skipping nearly all the way to Sights 'n' Sounds.

IT TOOK ONLY a minute to identify herself and collect her cassette player. The store owner even knew her, so there was no question of her identification. They took some pictures of her smiling and holding the prize. It all seemed terribly unreal to Stevie and totally wonderful.

"This is the most exciting thing that's ever happened to me, you know?" she said to the store manager, Ms. Weiss.

"It *is* pretty exciting," she said. "Even for us. We hope you'll enjoy that machine for years to come."

That sounded like a great idea to Stevie—except for one thing. She *couldn't* enjoy it until she had something to play on it. She needed at least one tape. And there she was, at the store where she could buy it. And she had her wallet in her pocket. And she had lots of money in her wallet. Still almost too excited to think, she walked over to the rock cassette section to choose. She clutched her prize with one hand while she flipped through the cassettes with the other.

What a day this was! Stevie promised herself she'd remember it—remember the wonderful feeling of winning—for a long time. She sighed contentedly and began her selection in earnest.

"I STILL ALMOST can't believe it," Stevie told Carole at their Saturday class. "I mean, I really *did* win a contest. I've been listening to tapes all week. You should hear the sound. It's fabulous!"

"Stevie!" Max called. The tone of his voice meant trouble. "This is no place for gossip," he said sternly. "This riding ring is for riding. Now to show the class how you've been paying attention, please demonstrate how to change diagonals at the trot."

At least Stevie knew how to do that. She squeezed Comanche gently with her legs and the horse picked up a trot. She rose with the trot when his right foreleg stepped forward. It was a completely natural, comfortable movement to her. She'd seen new riders struggle with it—including Lisa—but she was an experienced rider. Changing diagonals was easy for her. As Comanche came through the center of the ring and changed directions (just the way he was supposed to this time), she sat for one extra "beat" of his trot, and rose again, this time when his left foreleg stepped forward. She'd changed diagonals.

"Nice," Max said. From him, that was a very big compliment, and it might, just *might*, make up for his being annoyed at her talking in class.

She brought Comanche to the end of the line as the entire class followed her pattern, some better than others. Stevie was glad they were doing something she was already good at. She didn't have to pay too close attention and could think more about the neat music she'd been listening to since Tuesday. It was hard having at least two things you *really* liked doing—in this case, riding and listening to rock music—when you couldn't do them both at once. Then she realized that she'd be able to bring her cassette player on the MTO so they could all listen to music at their campsite at night. But which tapes would she bring? She couldn't bring them all, could she? She decided to ask Carole to help her choose. After all, the MTO was only two weeks away.

At last, class was almost over. They paired up for their final trot—this time through the center of the ring to change directions. She brought her horse up next to Carole's.

"Come to my house this afternoon? I've got

something really important to show you," Stevie invited her friend.

"I thought you'd have work to do. I was kind of planning to go to TD's with Lisa. Can she come over, too?"

Stevie frowned. She knew Carole was becoming Lisa's friend, but she couldn't forget that Lisa was the one who had tied her sneakers into all those knots. And Lisa was the one who wouldn't sit for the Ziegler twins when she'd needed somebody to do that job. And Lisa was the one—

"You know, Stevie, she thought you were the one who slammed the door when she was on Patch that first day."

"Is she crazy? What kind of person does she think I am?"

"Well, she knows better now, and she's really sorry about the sneakers—just like I'm sure *you're* sorry about the stirrups. Remember the stirrups?"

She did, of course. She remembered them well. She remembered how funny Lisa looked while she groped for a way to get on the horse. It was so funny, in fact, that she snickered now. But she also remembered that Lisa had been near tears. And she remembered that since that day, Lisa had learned a lot about horses and riding and had stuck with it, which a lot of new riders didn't.

"Okay, she can come," she said. "But what I want to talk about is the MTO. Is she going on it?"

"She and her mother are meeting with Max on Tuesday after class to talk about it. She wants to come and Max thinks she's learned enough to ride on a trail safely. Her mother's the problem."

"That's funny," Stevie said. "Max asked me if I could stay after class on Tuesday. He was a little mysterious about it."

"You don't think—" Carole began.

But they were interrupted then by the very person they were discussing. "Girls!" Max said very sternly. "Class is not over yet and I am the only one who is allowed to talk while class is in session. I cannot have you continue to break this rule. Do you understand?"

"Yes," they said in unison.

"NOW, LISTEN TO *this* one," Stevie said, sliding a cassette into her machine and fast-forwarding it expertly to the song she wanted to hear. She pressed play.

It was a wonderful song, Lisa thought. She'd heard it on the radio, but it sounded much better on Stevie's cassette player. It was a dreamy, romantic song. She leaned back in the comfortable overstuffed chair in Stevie's room to enjoy the music. It wasn't easy to relax, though. She felt like an intruder. She could tell that Carole was trying to make her like Stevie, and make Stevie like her, but it wasn't easy. Lisa's disastrous first day at Pine Hollow hung like a dark cloud between them. Lisa felt badly about the sneakers and she thought Stevie probably felt badly about the stirrups, but those things had happened, and it was going to be hard to forget them. She was trying, though. Hard. She wished Stevie would try, too.

"If you like this song, you're really going to like the next," Stevie said to Carole.

"Boy, you sure have a lot of tapes here," Carole said, shuffling through the selection. "I thought you didn't have any. Are these Alex's?"

"No, they're mine. I told you, he's got junky taste in music. He likes heavy metal. UGH!"

"Right!" Lisa agreed. It made her feel better that she and Stevie liked the same music.

"You bought them?" Carole asked suspiciously.

"Sure, they've got a good selection at Sights 'n' Sounds."

"You *bought* them?" Carole asked again. "Like you paid for them?"

"Sure I paid for them. They gave away a cassette player, but they didn't give me any tapes to go with it!"

"Where'd you get the money?" Carole challenged her.

"It was in my wallet. Hey, what did you think I did? Shoplift? No way. I can't believe you think I'd steal the tapes!" Stevie said, extremely agitated. "Look, here's the receipt!"

"Of course I don't think you stole them," Carole

said. "I know you'd never do anything dishonest. But I *am* worried that you spent every penny you had earned for the MTO to buy tapes!"

Stevie's arms dropped to her sides and she stood up, looking at Carole. She clutched a tape in her right hand. While Lisa watched, Stevie's face turned pale.

"No, I couldn't have done that. I had *lots* of money. I couldn't have spent it all. I only bought a few tapes—just those few you see there and two more that I've loaned to Alex for the day. That's all. There has to be a lot of money left. I mean, what does one tape cost?"

Lisa thought about the tapes she'd seen in the stores. They were pretty expensive. She counted eight tapes on Stevie's bed, plus the two Alex had. She supplied the answer to Stevie's question. "Ten tapes at six or seven dollars each. It's about sixty-five dollars, plus tax—"

"You spent *all* your money!" Carole yowled.

"Not all of it," Stevie said defensively. "I have some left." She grabbed her wallet from her purse and opened it. "I have exactly—" She dumped the contents on her bed. "Four dollars and eighteen cents."

Stevie was transformed before Lisa's eyes. The scene that followed made Stevie's ranting about the knots in her sneaker laces look like a picnic. Stevie was so furious with herself that she began grabbing all the papers on her desk and tossing them up in the air.

"I don't believe I did that! Can you believe it? Do

you know how many hours I worked and how I made one *zillion* phone calls—make that two zillion—to get jobs for everybody so I could earn a measly fifty dollars to do the one thing I really care about, which is to go on the MTO? I even sat for the Ziegler twins myself when I couldn't get anybody else. And what have I got to show for it?" A dozen slips of paper flew out of her right hand into the air. "Nothing!" She flung more paper toward the ceiling with her left hand. "And look at this!" She picked up her notebook. "Night after night was ruined because of the bookkeeping I had to do. *Look* at this!" She tossed the notebook toward the overstuffed chair where Lisa was sitting. It slammed onto the floor and slid under the chair's skirt.

When the first tears appeared in Stevie's eyes, Carole grabbed a tissue and went over to comfort her, but Stevie was inconsolable. The MTO was a once-in-a-lifetime trip. She'd wanted it so much that she'd done something she absolutely hated—she'd worked. And now she wasn't going to go anyway. "And it's all my fault!" Stevie wailed.

Lisa felt very bad for Stevie, but she was also a little embarrassed. After all, they weren't exactly close friends. While Carole comforted Stevie, Lisa retrieved the notebook from under the chair. Idly, she glanced at it. On the first double page, there was a neat chart. It only took a second to realize that it was Stevie's record book of the jobs she'd taken on. Until she looked at the record book, Lisa had no idea how much work had been done by Stevie, her brothers, and her friends. But the situation became clear as she glanced at the page in front of her. Across the top of the page were headings: Date, Job, Employer, Employee, Rate, Time, Amount Paid, Amount Due Employee, Amount Paid Employee, Commission. There were four pages like this, listing everything that had been done. That meant that a lot of jobs had been done. It was a tremendous amount of data.

In the back of the book were pages with the names of all the kids who had worked for her. Stevie had made careful notes about them. On Polly Giacomin's page, for example, it said, "Orthodontist on Wednesdays. Mrs. Ellerman says she was good with the dog." There was a page with her own name on it. "Lisa Atwood," it said. "Didn't seem interested." It made her uncomfortable to read it. But it was true, of course. Stevie had asked her to sit and she wasn't interested. She'd given her an excuse about studying for a test, but Stevie had obviously known it was just an excuse. Then there was Carole's page. It said, "Will do anything for Cobalt. Natch." That was true, too, Lisa knew.

She looked up from the notebook. Stevie was sniffling. "I'll take the cassettes back," Stevie said, gathering them up, and trying to sort cassettes and cases. "I'll tell the store they were damaged and demand my money back."

"Stevie!" Carole said, a little exasperated.

Suddenly, Lisa got a wonderful idea. "Uh, Stevie?" Lisa tried to interrupt. Stevie didn't hear her.

"I'll tell them my family's fortune was wiped out by a tornado and we are desperate for cash."

"Stevie," Lisa said again. No luck.

"A hurricane, maybe—"

"Stevie! Get yourself together, girl," Carole chided.

"Listen, Carole," Lisa said, clutching the notebook. Carole didn't hear her, either, because she was so busy with Stevie.

"Stevie, you only have one choice," Carole told her in a matter-of-fact tone of voice. "You *have* to do a math project."

"No!" Stevie wailed. "I *can't!*"

It was Lisa's chance. "Yes!" she wailed, imitating Stevie's cry. "You already *have!*"

"Have what?" Stevie asked, looking bewildered.

"Have a math project," Lisa said.

"What do you mean?" Stevie asked, suddenly interested.

"Here," Lisa said, pointing to the notebook. "You have a math project. You said you did a lot of work. And you did. But you also did a math project when you started keeping this ledger."

Stevie started listening. She sat down on the bed facing Lisa and pulled her knees up to her chin. Carole sat next to her, dangling her legs over the edge of the bed.

"Look, you're supposed to do a project on percentages and decimals, right?" Lisa continued.

Stevie nodded.

"Well, what's more decimal than dollars and cents and what's more percentage than commissions?"

Stevie nodded, a slow smile spreading across her face.

"So, all you have to do is make sure you've got all the jobs entered, finish doing the arithmetic, and do some analytical percentages, like such and such percent of the employers paid on the spot. Such and such percent never paid. You got such and such percent of the money. The average job paid so much money, et cetera. The math isn't hard. You can even use a calculator. The only hard part is making sure you have all the information. Where are your records on the other jobs?"

"Other jobs?" Stevie asked.

"Yeah, this stuff only goes through Friday a week ago. I know other jobs have been done since then and there are some blanks before that. Where are your records?"

Stevie looked up to the ceiling and then down to the floor. The entire floor was scattered with the scraps of paper she'd thrown in the air when she was so angry.

"Oh, no," Stevie groaned.

"Oh, no!" Carole said.

"Well, there's just one thing to do," Lisa announced. "And that is to pick them up and start working on Stevie's math project. We can't have her at home alone while we're enjoying the MTO, can we, Carole?"

"No, we cannot," Carole agreed, lowering herself to the floor. She began picking up crumpled and torn scraps of paper.

Lisa and Stevie got onto the floor as well. There was still a lot of work ahead of them—and when a big job needed to be done, it was better if friends did it together.

CAROLE SPOTTED LISA in the main-floor hall of the school between her science and gym classes on Monday morning. She knew right away it was Lisa because of the perfectly pressed blouse and matching skirt. Lisa's mother still liked to dress her up like a doll. Carole wondered when Mrs. Atwood would start letting Lisa make her own decisions.

"Hey, Lisa, wait up!" she yelled, running down the hall. Lisa stopped and smiled when she saw her. Or maybe she was smiling because of the trail of papers Carole had dropped behind her. They picked them up together.

"How's it going?" Carole asked eagerly. She knew that Lisa had spent most of Sunday at Stevie's, working on Project Math Project, as they'd dubbed their joint effort.

"It's going okay, sort of. You wouldn't believe the amount of work Stevie did. When she said she'd made a zillion phone calls, she was only slightly exaggerating! And just during the time I was there, she had at least ten more calls—"

"Did she take the jobs?"

"No, she told people she was out of business. A lot of her customers seemed very disappointed, too, but we had a giant pile of work to do so she couldn't spend any more time on the phone getting workers."

"How big a giant pile? I mean, like it's due on Friday. Is she going to get it done on time?"

"With a little help from her friends," Lisa said. "Really, it's going to be a terrific report, someday."

"By Friday?" The question hung in the air. Lisa shrugged. "You know what I think?" Carole continued. "If Stevie could do all that work to earn the money, she can certainly account for it all so the three of us can go on the MTO."

"Well, that's another thing," Lisa said, ominously. Suddenly, Carole got the feeling that a bombshell was coming. "My mother is getting convinced that there's no way I can be trusted on a three-day trail ride. I mean, at first, she really wanted me to ride because that's what well-bred people supposedly do." Lisa grimaced. "But then, she met the sainted Veronica, who was a real jerk when she was at my house. Now Mom thinks too much riding isn't a good idea for a young lady. Besides, she thinks three days in the mountains sounds too rough. So, Stevie may be able to go. But I probably won't."

Just when Carole had thought things were looking up, she found out they weren't.

On Monday afternoon, Lisa was back at Stevie's, piecing together the scraps of information that would someday be a math project.

"Okay, then, you had three jobs going on the afternoon of the twentieth. But I don't understand how you've got 'Alex' down for all of them. I mean, I know he's terrific and all, being your twin brother, but he's not exactly Superman, is he?"

"No, he's not," Stevie said. "But he must have done the jobs if I said he did."

"Well, here, you look at these slips of paper. Isn't that what these say?" She handed Stevie the crumpled pieces of paper with notes scribbled on them. Stevie took them reluctantly. It seemed to her that in the last two days all she'd been doing was staring at crumpled notes—in her own messy handwriting.

"No, no, this isn't Alex," she said once she'd decoded her scratchings. "It's Alex*a*. That's Alexa Hammond, our neighbor. She's a demon in the kitchen. That's why I had her work with Mrs. Alcott—"

"But you said Mrs. Alcott was the one who never paid you and you've got this marked 'Paid.'"

"Well, I mean, I paid Alexa. It's just that Mrs. Alcott hasn't paid me. Or at least she hadn't then. I'm pretty sure she did pay me. I know I wrote a note about it."

Lisa sighed. "If you made a note of it, we'll find it." For now, that closed the subject. Lisa concentrated on the notebook on the desk in front of her. Stevie watched her, amazed at Lisa's ability to concentrate totally on something so dull. While Stevie watched her, Lisa reached for the pencil behind her right ear—no doubt changing "Alex" to "Alexa."

"Should I get us some sodas?" Stevie asked.

"Hmmm," was all she got in reply. Lisa was so focused on the notebook that Stevie doubted she'd heard her at all. Quietly, she left the room. As she scouted for sodas and cookies in the kitchen, she mused at the generosity of a friend—and she knew now that Lisa *was* a friend—who would spend so much time helping another girl with schoolwork.

She pulled two straws out of their box and returned to her room, determined to concentrate as hard as Lisa. Together, she was sure they could do the project—as sure as she'd been that she could earn the fifty dollars. She'd been right about that, too, she thought just a little smugly.

* * *

ON TUESDAY AFTERNOON, Carole wasn't certain whether she wanted her riding class to end or to go on forever. She was very aware of the fact that both of her friends had been summoned to Max's office after class, and she'd noted the arrival of Mrs. Atwood. According to Lisa, Mrs. Atwood was still determined that her daughter should not go on the MTO. Carole thought that was weird since it was Mrs. Atwood who had insisted Lisa take riding lessons in the first place. Lisa was equally determined to go. Carole had had one or two opportunities to see Lisa face up to her mother, especially that first day Lisa had come to Pine Hollow. She wasn't really very good at standing up to her mother, Carole thought glumly.

And then there was Stevie. If Stevie ever did finish her math project, she'd still have trouble convincing Max to let her go after the way she'd been acting in class recently. She'd even been late today, saying she'd had to stop and borrow a calculator from a friend before riding class. Being late to class was one of Max's pet peeves. But just one of them. He had loads, and these days it seemed that every time Carole turned around, Max was yelling at Stevie for one thing or another.

After class, Carole finished untacking Delilah, and then checked to see that Veronica had given Cobalt fresh water. She hadn't, of course, so Carole did it for her. Then she returned Delilah's tack to the tack room, where she'd decided to wait for the results of her friends' powwow with Max.

But just exactly *what* was going on? Why were Lisa, her mother, and Stevie in there all at once? Was Max just letting both of them know at the same time that they couldn't go on the MTO?

"Carole, what's on your mind, child?" Mrs. Reg asked gently as she poked her head through the tack-room door.

"Oh, nothing," Carole said as vaguely as she could, trying not to look toward Max's office.

"Well, I can't believe there's nothing on your mind when I see you putting Delilah's tack away upside down. And you can't convince me you're not worried about something when I watched you rinse out Cobalt's bucket six times—*after* you'd filled it once."

Carole smiled weakly. "That obvious, huh?"

"Yes, it is. Now straighten out the tack and come tell me what's bothering you so."

Carole was relieved to have a chance to talk about her worries. Probably Mrs. Reg couldn't change anything, but maybe just talking about it all would help. She turned Delilah's bridle right side up, straightened out the saddle, and went to sit on the bench near Mrs. Reg's desk.

"It's my friends," she began.

"They've been hurting your feelings?" Mrs. Reg asked. Her bright blue eyes flashed in anger on Carole's behalf.

"Oh, no. They've been hurting themselves," Carole explained, even though she knew it didn't make very much sense. "I've tried and tried to help them, but I'm just so afraid that it isn't enough. If I could just—" Carole let the words hang in the air. She didn't know how to finish the sentence. What, after all, *could* she do for her friends?

"Now, wait a minute," Mrs. Reg said. "There's only so much you can do for friends, Carole. And sometimes, the best thing you can do is to let them do something for themselves. I remember I had a horse once—a beauty, he was. The tack that came with him included a really harsh bit." Carole knew that meant that every time the rider put pressure on the reins, the horse would really feel it. Even the wildest horse would have trouble ignoring a command from a tough bit.

"Anyway," Mrs. Reg continued, "each time I rode that horse, I kept giving him firmer signals with the reins and the bit. We had a very uncomfortable relationship, you know. Then one day, the bit broke. The only extra one around was a jointed snaffle. I figured it would be a disaster to ride with it because the snaffle is so gentle. But I had to exercise the horse, so I tried it. It was like night and day, I'll tell you. That horse had known all along what it was he was supposed to do: It was just that he didn't like the way I was trying to control him. When he had a little bit of freedom, he did just exactly the right thing."

"I guess I shouldn't interfere so much in my friends' lives, huh?" Carole asked after a pause.

"No, that's not exactly what I mean, Carole. I think you should give people the help they need, but when it comes to the things they have to do by themselves, let them do it. Good friends always come through."

"Always?"

"Well, usually," Mrs. Reg corrected herself.

"Thanks, Mrs. Reg," Carole said as the older woman left the tack room. Still, she didn't feel comforted. It was one thing for her friends to do the right thing. It was another to expect either Mrs. Atwood or Max to do the right thing.

What *were* they all doing in his office for so long?

"SEE YOU LATER, Mom." Lisa's voice emerged from the silence. Carole sat up straight. She could practically hear her heart beat, she was so nervous about the outcome of this big meeting. She knew that Lisa and Stevie would be in the tack room in a minute. They had arranged to meet there before class. She stared at the door, barely able to contain her excitement. She strained to hear Lisa's and Stevie's footsteps.

The door opened and Stevie and Lisa appeared, solemn-faced. Then, as Carole watched, bewildered, the two of them exchanged glances and waited for the door to close soundly behind them. When it was shut, they both jumped up in the air and yelled "Yahoooooo!" at the same time.

It could only mean one thing—victory!

"What happened? Are you going? Both of you?" Carole could barely get the questions out fast enough.

"You bet we are," Stevie said positively. "Max was just great—he was wonderful. I'm telling you, Carole, he was fantastic. I didn't know he would do such a thing, but he was *outstanding.*"

"What happened?" Carole asked, practically dying of curiosity.

"You tell, Lisa. She's your mother," Stevie said, passing the honors on to her friend.

"Oh, Max was great," Lisa said.

"I know that. We all know that," Carole said. "Just what did he *do?*"

"He convinced my mother to let me go on the MTO on the grounds that Stevie would be my partner."

"Stevie?" Carole asked. Stevie was a good rider and all, but no doubt about it, Carole was the best rider in the class. If Lisa needed a partner, which, in Carole's opinion, she did not, Carole would have been the likely candidate.

"How come Stevie?" Carole asked, feeling a little hurt.

"Because he told her that Lisa was helping me with my math project. And then he told her I'd asked him for a chance to help Lisa with something in return. That was news to me, but it worked! Lisa's mother thought that was a great idea. So did I!"

Suddenly, Carole saw the light. Max had maneuvered Mrs. Atwood into letting Lisa come on the MTO! He was something else.

"Max did this with a straight face?" Carole asked.

"Just *barely,*" Stevie admitted. Suddenly the three girls were overcome with relief and joy. Carole started giggling first, and then Stevie burst into laughter. In seconds, Lisa was laughing along with them both and then the three of them hugged each other with joy.

"Yahoooooo!" Carole cried.

That said it all.

Just at that moment, the door to the tack room opened and Veronica diAngelo sauntered in. Carole was surprised to see her there so late after class.

"I had to talk to Max about *private* jumping lessons," Veronica said, explaining her presence. She sat down on the bench to remove her riding boots. "And what are *you* doing here so late?" she asked.

"We were talking to Max about the MTO," Lisa volunteered. "And he said I could go—and Stevie will be my partner! Isn't that great?"

"Oh, sure, great," Veronica said. She didn't sound

like she meant it at all. Veronica finished changing her shoes, then stood up and left the tack room as regally as she had entered it.

As soon as the door closed, the three girls burst into giggles.

"Oh, sure, great!" Stevie mimicked Veronica. "Did you ever hear such insincerity?"

"What made you tell her?" Carole asked Lisa.

Lisa thought for a moment. "I think I wanted her to know that Max believes I'm a good enough rider to go on the MTO when she didn't think I was a good enough rider to be her friend."

"Well, I'll tell you one thing," Stevie said.

"What?"

"Not only are you a good enough rider to be *my* friend, but you're also a great math student and I think it's time to get back to work on Project Math Project—due in three days!" She paused for a second and then went on. "You know, today I feel so good, I could add up a column of fifty-six numbers and not make a mistake!"

"Let's not waste a second, then!" Lisa teased. "Let's go!"

Together, the three of them headed for Stevie's house.

"NOW, STEVIE, HERE'S how you set up the problems. If you do the math, I'll fill in your answers on the work sheet. We don't have all the information—we *know* some stuff is definitely missing, but you've got to start the calculations," Lisa told her in a very businesslike manner.

Stevie took the paper and calculator and sat at her desk to begin her work—nearly the final steps of the project.

Neither Stevie nor Lisa was aware of Carole. She was sprawled under Stevie's bed where she'd chased Stevie's cat, Madonna, who'd run off with her pen. In the dim light, Carole could see that the cat was crouched over a pile of little crumpled bits of paper. Madonna cocked her right front paw and began batting one of the pieces of balled-up paper. It skittered across the floor, and the cat pounced on it with glee.

Carole laughed at Madonna's antics. The cat attacked another ball of crumpled paper, while Carole watched, fascinated. Then it struck her! "Eureka!" she yelled.

"Don't distract me—I'm adding up a whole bunch of numbers," Stevie said irritably.

"Hold it a second," Carole said, knowing her voice was muffled under the bed. She waddled backwards to get out. As she moved, she collected Madonna's cache of paper balls and brought them with her. "You've got to stop adding that column because I think—if my eyes and brain haven't deceived me—that you have a whole bunch more to add in!" Proudly, Carole displayed her booty.

Lisa gasped. "The missing data!" She grabbed for the papers.

"Oh, no! More numbers to add!" Stevie groaned.

"But now we have everything," Lisa said, trying to comfort her. She smoothed out each scrap of paper, deciphering Stevie's scribbles—something she'd had an awful lot of practice doing over the last few days.

Stevie sighed, but she took the papers and methodically began adding them to her work sheets. There was a lot more work to do, but Stevie seemed determined to do it. Carole just hoped she could do it by bedtime tonight. The report was due first thing in the morning.

A few hours later, it was all done. The final calculation had been entered, the final analysis made, the last penny accounted for.

"I hope I get the grade I need on this. I don't think I've ever worked harder on something for school than I did on this," Stevie said, staring at the finished product.

"Me, neither," Lisa said. "Even on something of my own!"

The next morning, Stevie was out of bed early. She wanted to have one last look at her math project. That project represented not only a lot of work on her part—and her friends', as well—but it was almost as if it *were* the MTO. She reached for the cover to open it, but her hand stopped. She didn't dare look inside. What if it looked awful to her this morning? It was better not to know.

Later that Friday morning, she put it on her teacher's desk and walked to her own seat. She never looked back, but at that moment, she had the feeling she understood why her mother had behaved so strangely the first day Michael had gone off to nursery school. The project was her baby.

She crossed her fingers.

ON SATURDAY, THE three girls had riding class together. They were working on the proper way to sit in the saddle at a canter.

Lisa was really glad that it was hard to do because it

would have been impossible to concentrate on anything easy.

"Now slide in the saddle, rock with the horse, Lisa!" Max said. "And don't hold on!" Lisa let go of the front of the saddle and tried to slide. "Relax!" Max said. How could she relax? She tried it. It didn't work. She didn't feel relaxed about Stevie, but she must have been a little more relaxed about cantering. "Good, Lisa," Max said. "Much better." That was how much *he* knew.

ON MONDAY AFTER school, the call came. Carole had been waiting to hear from Stevie for so long that she was beginning to think she'd miss the waiting when it was over. But that was silly, of course.

"I got it back," Stevie said as soon as Carole answered the phone.

"And?" Carole said, the phone pressed tightly to her ear.

"I can barely say it," Stevie said.

"Say *what*?" Carole asked, fearing the worst.

Stevie cleared her throat. "A-plus. I got an A-plus on my math report."

Carole whooped with joy.

"That means that my term grade is now going to be a B-plus. That's the best I've done in math since third grade! Can you believe it? It's true!"

"Wow," Carole uttered in relief. "That's wonderful. Congratulations. Have you called Lisa?"

"I already did," Stevie said. "After all, I couldn't possibly have done it without her. And she's invited you and me to come over to her house Saturday after class for a celebration. Okay with you?"

"Great with me," Carole said, grinning broadly. "Saturday will be great. I'll see you tomorrow at class."

And when she hung up the phone, Carole shouted "Yahooooo!"

"What's got you so excited, baby?" her father called from the living room.

"Oh—just everything, Daddy. Everything's great! Say, Daddy, what's round and purple and gets A-pluses on her math projects?"

Not surprisingly, her father didn't answer.

"Stevie the Grape," Carole said, giggling to herself.

"OKAY, SO YOU don't think I should take a dress," Lisa said jokingly.

"Only if it's a designer dress and your mother insists," Stevie teased her. Lisa grinned in response. The three girls were gathered in Lisa's room, chatting happily about the MTO, deciding what to take with them.

"I guess I will be able to take my cassette player after all," Stevie said.

"Right, but don't bring along any music that will frighten the horses," Carole said. "Just something that will frighten Veronica—"

"Hey, great idea! Maybe I'll see if I can buy a tape of creepy night sounds. I still have some money left and, after all, Betsy owes me some from that job she did."

Lisa gave her a look. "If you don't mind, Stevie, I think that today should be the end of all talk about anything to do with the *math* project."

"Okay," Stevie said agreeably. "So today is the end of one thing—and the beginning of another. But what's it the beginning of?"

"The MTO," Lisa said.

"No," Stevie contradicted her. "The MTO starts next Friday afternoon and goes for the entire holiday weekend. Today is the start of something else, I think, but what?"

Both girls looked over at Carole, who was sitting in the overstuffed chair by the window. "Carole, you with us?" Lisa asked gently.

Carole nodded. "You know, I just keep thinking how lucky I am to have two friends like you," she said.

"Now, don't get sappy on me," Stevie teased.

"I wouldn't do that," Carole said, grinning. "I'm just happy, but also a little amazed. I mean, I think it would be hard for me to find two girls who are so different from me—and from each other. But we're all friends."

They all paused to think. "I mean, we've got Stevie the practical joker—" Carole continued.

"Who promises not to do any jokes at her friends' expense," Stevie said solemnly.

"Then there's Lisa, the straight-A student who—"

"Helps Stevie ace her math project," Lisa said.

"And Carole the flake who misses buses and scatters

papers. But who can find the critical piece of paper under Stevie's bed at just the right moment." Carole paused. They all looked at one another, more pleased than distressed at their differences.

"But," Carole continued, "we also have something in common. Something very important to each of us. We all love horses. We love riding them, we love training them, we love taking care of them."

"Well, I'm not crazy about mucking out stalls," Stevie corrected Carole.

"I never said you were crazy," Carole teased her. "I just said you were *horse* crazy. We all are, aren't we?"

"You bet," Lisa agreed. Stevie nodded as well.

"Okay, so how about this? Today marks the beginning of The Saddle Club. All you have to do to belong is to be a friend to the other members, which may include things like helping on math projects, or saddling difficult horses, or promising to be a partner on an overnight trip—and you have to be horse crazy, right?"

"But mostly you have to be horse crazy?" Stevie suggested. She didn't want to do another math project.

"Mostly," Carole agreed.

First, they all shook on it. And then they all hugged. Each knew that being horse crazy was going to be great.

"To The Saddle Club!" Lisa said, lifting her soda can high into the air.

"To The Saddle Club!" her friends echoed, clinking their sodas against hers.

It was a wonderful sound.

ABOUT THE AUTHOR

BONNIE BRYANT is the author of more than twenty-five books for young readers, including the best-selling novelizations of *The Karate Kid* movies. The Saddle Club books were her first especially written for Bantam Books. Her new series, Pony Tails, is already enjoying great success and is set to follow in the footsteps, or should I say hoof-marks, of The Saddle Club.

Whenever she can, Ms Bryant goes horseback riding in her hometown, New York City. She's had many riding experiences in the city's Central Park that have found their way into her Saddle Club books – and lots which haven't!

Bonnie has two sons, and they live together in an apartment in Greenwich Village that is just too small for a horse.